Love at
FIRST SOUND

Amaka Azie

First Published in Great Britain in 2019 by
LOVE AFRICA PRESS
103 Reaver House, 12 East Street, Epsom KT17 1HX
www.loveafricapress.com

LOVE AFRICA
PRESS
African Love Stories

ISBN: 978-1-9161546-0-5
Also available as eBook

CHAPTER ONE

Yomi Oladipo loosened his tie as he pushed opened the door of his two-bedroom apartment. Another long day, and he couldn't wait to kick back and unwind with a bottle of Chardonnay while listening to his favourite radio show.

The loud buzzing of his mobile phone jarred him, and the paper pack of roasted corn he'd ordered on his way back home almost slipped from his hand.

Sighing, he reached into his pocket and retrieved his phone. He swiped a thumb across the screen, and the cheerful image of his brother lit the display.

"Damn it, Kunle. You call at the most annoying times," he grumbled, holding the phone upright in one hand while awkwardly juggling his takeaway meal and briefcase in the other.

"Bro, I can see you keep to your tradition of roasted corn every Friday night. And I guess the next thing is to listen to your wife on the radio."

"Shut up," Yomi snickered, chuckling. "She isn't my wife. And I'm still happily single, thank you very much."

"Just say you love her. For the past five years, you've never missed her show. And you've just purchased her new book. I bet you wish she wasn't anonymous, so you could find her and marry her already."

Yomi laughed. He agreed with his brother. Yes, he wanted to meet Sasha, the radio relationship and sex therapist. Her show had captivated him from the very first day he'd listened to it. There was something about her voice and the direct way she gave her advice that

3

had caught his attention, kept him hooked. But he wasn't about to admit all that to Kunle.

"Big bro, I'm sure you didn't call me just to badger me."

"Of course I didn't." He hesitated, cleared his throat, and puffed out a sigh. "I called ... I wanted to talk about Mum ..."

He became still. The mention of his mother caused his stomach to plummet.

"Please don't. I've told you that woman is dead to me—"

"Don't say that, Yomi. She is your mother."

"No, she isn't." He seethed. "No woman who abandons her children to run off with her lover deserves to be called a mother. Nope. She's not my mother." His blood boiled as he spoke.

"Yomi—"

"Kunle ... Please. Don't. If you want to remain in contact with her, that's your choice. But don't try to involve me in that mess."

"She is in town, Yomi. She wants to see you."

"Well, that isn't going to happen. She can crawl back to London with her toy boy and leave me the fuck alone. I don't want to see her. Not now. Not ever. So, forget it and never mention her to me again."

Bile rose to his throat. The image of his beautiful mother—blonde, blue-eyed, and dainty as a feather—half-dressed and moaning loudly as she rode astride a young dark-skinned stranger barely out of his teens, scorched Yomi's brain.

Still as fresh as when he'd witnessed it at the age of seventeen. He would never forget the shock of betrayal that had pierced his chest when he had stridden into the sitting room of the family home and unexpectedly discovered her infidelity. No, he wanted nothing to do with that adulterous excuse for a mother.

4

"Okay ... okay." Kunle's tone sounded resigned. "Didn't mean to ruin your evening."

Lowering his briefcase to the ground beside him, Yomi blew out a regretful breath, a bit ashamed of his outburst. He hadn't meant to yell at his older brother. Although only a two-year age gap existed between them, he had deep respect for him.

"I'm sorry for yelling," he said. Then, he stretched his lips into a smile to show his brother his remorse and continued. "And you didn't ruin my evening. Nobody can ruin my Fridays because my wife on the radio always takes away my stress."

His brother laughed out loud, the tension between them immediately forgotten. "Aha! Now you admit you are spiritually married to her," Kunle chortled. "Sasha—the only person with the power to soothe you."

Yomi nodded. "Okay, I admit it. I love Sasha's voice—if that's her real name. And her guts. I mean, there is something to be said about being a bold radio sex therapist ..."

"Not so bold, though. She remains anonymous."

"Yeah ... yeah ... I don't blame her. With all the creeps in Lagos, I think that's a wise decision. Idiotic people may assume she is promiscuous because she's a sex therapist and cause her grief."

"You're right." Kunle yawned, triggering an answering yawn in Yomi, too.

"Okay, Kunle. Speaking of which ... it's almost time for the show, and I need to get my dinner ready before it starts."

"Corn isn't dinner." Kunle snorted. "Keep eating that, and you'll end up severely constipated," he said with a dismissive wave of one hand. "Talk to you later."

Yomi smiled. "Okay, later."

After hanging up, he made his way to the efficient but spacious kitchen adjacent to the sitting room. He pulled out two corn cobs from newspaper wraps and placed them on a plate. Whistling softly, he retrieved a small bowl containing chopped pieces of coconut from the fridge and placed both items on a silver tray, after which he lifted a chilled bottle of wine.

His entire body pulsated with anticipation as he moved back to the sitting room, balancing the tray effortlessly in both hands. With a deep sigh of satisfaction, he slumped on the recliner and switched on the radio.

The digital clock hanging on the bright white wall read eleven p.m.

"Right on time," he muttered, lifting a cob of corn to his lips and biting down on it.

"Welcome, lovers. It's so great to be back again for *Late Nights with Sasha* at Mainland FM 106.2."

The sultry voice from the radio resounded in the room, seeping slowly from his ears down his body like sweet caramel syrup dripping down a tasty treat.

"For a mature audience only. So, if you are less than eighteen years old, close your ears." She let out a soft giggle that sent a jolt of awareness coursing through him. "Here, you get all the tips you need to keep your relationship spicy and your sex life steamy. Ring the number 090 237 237 with any questions you have about love, sex, and relationships, and I'll do my best to answer."

Slow rhythm and blues music followed her sultry pronouncement, breaking through his trance.

Yomi exhaled the breath he hadn't realised he'd been holding. It still amazed him how much effect Sasha's voice had on him, even leaving him spellbound sometimes.

"We have our first caller," she spoke again, cutting through the music. "Hello, you are through to *Late Nights with Sasha*. What's your name, and what's your question?"

"Thanks for taking my call, Sasha. My name is Amaka—" A loud screech emanated from the stereo, causing Yomi to wince.

"Amaka, nice to have you call in. Can you turn down your radio, so we can hear you properly?"

Silence for a few seconds, and then—"Can you hear me now?"

"Yes, that's fantastic," Sasha said, her voice low and husky, like a warm caress over his skin. "So, Amaka, how can I help?"

"Oh ... I am a bit embarrassed about this ... Okay, so, my husband brought some sex toys for our tenth wedding anniversary celebration getaway. And to be honest, I ... I feel betrayed. Why would he feel the need to bring that filth into our matrimonial bed?" A second of hesitation. "Should I be worried he's cheating on me? No longer satisfied with our sex life?"

Yomi sat up, anticipating Sasha's reply. Although he had heard her clever responses to difficult questions such as this before, he still looked forward to every word she uttered like a student listening to a lecture a day before exams.

"Great, Amaka, I love your honesty. And I'm glad you called. My answer to your first question is that I feel it's unlikely that your husband is cheating if he is willing to try new things with you in the bedroom. From my experience as a psychologist, when a person gives up on a relationship, they don't bother dealing with important issues like sex with their partners. They simply go elsewhere to find what they need."

Yomi nodded vigorously as she spoke.

"Absolutely correct, Sasha!" he said to no one.

"And my answer to your second question is, yes. He probably wants more from your sex life and wants to spice things up with you. I actually think that's a good thing."

"Oh, I didn't see it that way." Amaka's tone wavered, sounding surprised, as though she'd expected Sasha to reflect the repulsion she felt about her husband's request. "But sex toys, though ... I have never used them ... I find them ... I don't know ... sinful."

"You are not alone, Amaka. It's common for women and men to feel worried about anything being introduced to conventional sexual activity. Even non-conventional sexual positions are shocking to many people. So, don't feel isolated."

"Really?"

"Of course."

"So, what do I do about this sex toy thing? I'm not sure I want to use them ... or even know how to."

"I think you should talk with your husband. Find out what he feels about your sex life. Study the sex toys, find out how they are used, if you are comfortable with what they do."

Yomi nodded again, totally impressed by Sasha's insight. "Preach, my sweet Sasha! Preach."

"Try them on yourself, then try them with your husband if you're happy with the results," Sasha said. Her husky chuckle came seconds after. "Maybe you would get to love them so much that you want to use them every time."

A loud gasp resounded from the speakers. Likely from Amaka. "Ah ... Sasha. I'm not so sure."

"Nobody is ever sure about anything until they try it, honey. Don't knock it until you do."

"Thanks, Sasha. I'll think about it."

"Thanks for calling, Amaka, I'm happy to have helped. One more thing before you go ... Remember, nothing is sinful unless you want it to be."

The sound of instrumental jazz floated into the room. "Lovers, keep that dial tuned to Mainland FM 106.2 as we go into a brief commercial break."

Yomi settled back onto his seat and took a sip from his glass of wine. Oh, he would give anything to meet Sasha. His brother was right. He'd fallen in love with the sound of her voice without even knowing what she looked like. How crazy was that?

CHAPTER TWO

Streaks of sweat sleeked down Emem's back. Her stomach tightened in knots as she eyed her reflection in the mirror.

"You can do this," she whispered, rolling the pen nestled between her thumb and index fingers. "You've planned this for eight weeks. Don't fall apart now."

She focused her attention on the image of herself staring back at her. Although she wouldn't call herself classically beautiful, she had smooth dark brown skin with no blemishes. Her eyelashes were thick and long, engendering the constant envy of her friends. Her nose, though small, flared slightly at the sides, and she could boast of full lips and a flawless smile—her most striking feature, she'd been told. "You should be on a toothpaste commercial. You have a perfect smile."—a compliment that had been repeatedly given to her for years.

Only, for the past few weeks, there'd hardly been any need to show her even white teeth. Like a robot, she'd been going through the motions of living as though a terrible discovery wasn't weighing heavily on her mind.

Dragging in a sorrowful breath, she ran a hand over the short-cropped curls on her head.

Maybe he cheated because I cut my hair.

The thought came again. Like it had done repeatedly since she'd found out her fiancé was also engaged to someone else. No matter how hard she'd tried, it seemed almost impossible to shake off that nagging worry that she could have done something to prevent it.

Maybe if she'd been more attentive, sexier, tried to be more of a homemaker, sucked up to his mother like he'd wanted her to, and definitely maybe if she hadn't cut her hair—just maybe if she still left it chemically straightened, long and flowing down her shoulders, Ejike wouldn't have strayed.

Emem shook her head at her own foolishness. *Ludicrous.* She twisted her lips. *Blaming your hair now, are you? Really?*

As a trained psychologist and relationship counsellor, she usually helped other people with issues like this and knew that blaming herself for the actions of another person was completely outrageous. But knowing better didn't stop her from condemning herself.

For the past five months since she had found evidence of Ejike's engagement to another woman, she'd lain awake beside him, thinking about what to do with the information. Yet, he'd remained the same. No inclination from his demeanour or behaviour that he had another life in America. All his business trips were just a ruse to continue living that double life.

Sucking air deep into her lungs, she fought back the tears that burned the back of her eyes. No, she wouldn't cry. Her tears had been overwhelming the first few days after her discovery. Then, those tears had led to confusion, denial, and finally, anger.

She couldn't allow herself to be drawn back to sorrow. The grieving process was supposed to move forward and not backwards. Nonetheless, she couldn't help but feel that she had reached rock bottom. Her heart now closed up, there could be no letting any other man in the way she'd let Ejike.

Since they'd met five years ago, she'd fallen hard for him, built her life around him, given up so much of herself. Even quit her job at a prominent TV station and moved away from Port Harcourt, where her family lived, to start a life with him in Lagos just because he'd been transferred here. She'd also remained anonymous because he was embarrassed about dating a radio sex talk show host, and worst of all, had lost a part of her body because she'd found herself carrying his baby when he hadn't been ready for a family.

Emem lowered a hand to her belly and shook her head. No point dwelling on that painful period of her life. The entire five years with him had left her with nothing. No marriage, no children, nothing! Well ... she could still have her dignity, and that's why she needed to do this.

Exhaling slowly, she lowered her pen to the clear A4 sheet of paper in front of the dressing table where she sat.

Dear Ejike,

I know you are engaged to Sally Ezumba and that your wedding is in 3 weeks. Congratulations. And also, on her pregnancy.

I am leaving you. Please don't think I'm angry. I wish you all the best. Don't try to find me. Just move on and have a good life with your wife filled with lots of love and happiness.

The joint account has been dissolved too. Half of the money is yours.

Best wishes

Emem

She read the note again, unable to believe how polite she sounded when all she wanted to do was tell him to jump off a cliff with his skinny, much younger fiancée in America. Oh, how she hated that the woman seemed so sweet and lovely in videos and pictures she'd seen of her on Instagram.

A new graduate in her early twenties, Sally looked like the woman Ejike wanted her to be. '*Why are you so opinionated? Why can't you just listen to my mother? Why did you cut your hair? You need to cook more. We can't keep ordering takeout meals. Are you getting fat?*' He'd kept them coming. Criticisms upon criticisms. And although they'd always hurt her, she'd repeatedly blamed herself for the disparagement.

No matter how hard she'd tried, Ejike had never seemed happy with her efforts. Now, she knew why. He had found what he'd always wanted. A younger, virginal damsel possessing all the pliability he desired. While she, a thirty-eight-year-old, emotionally damaged woman with half a reproductive system, was no longer of any use to him.

Tears gathered in her eyes, and she closed them tightly to keep them from falling. Nope. She couldn't shed one more tear for him. She couldn't afford to. Her family would only say, "I told you so." And she wasn't prepared to hear that from them, from anyone. When she eventually went back home to Port Harcourt, it had to be with a carefree attitude. So that nobody would suspect that Ejike had broken her heart.

Time to start a life on her own, work on building her career, and becoming the best damned radio show host in Nigeria. Maybe even get back to doing some clinical psychology sessions like she used to, before moving to Lagos. Have something to show for her years away from home. No more distractions.

After inserting the pictures of Ejike and Sally's engagement party she'd printed off from the Internet into a large brown envelope, Emem sealed it and placed her hand-written note atop it. She pulled herself up from her seat, sauntered over to the bed, and placed both onto the king-size mattress.

She scanned the room with her gaze and sighed in satisfaction. The large bed she'd slept on with Ejike for the past few years was well made. The silver and gold embroidery curtains draping the freshly cleaned windows were neatly anchored at the corners. Every sentimental ornament she'd purchased with him to build a home together stood as perfectly placed as they'd been when the interior decorator had worked on this room.

Back then, she'd felt so much promise with Ejike. A future, a life. A regretful sigh escaped her lips.

"Bye, dreams," she muttered as she reached into the purse hanging down her shoulder and pulled out her mobile phone. She slid her finger across the small screen until she located the number she needed and pressed down the dial symbol.

"Natalie," she said as soon as the line connected. "I'm ready. Please come get me."

***

Yomi sprang upright in bed. Disoriented, he glanced around his bedroom, his eyes still hazy from sleep and unable to focus on anything. A loud bang resounded again. Like the sound of a metal object hitting the ground.

What the fuck?

He jumped up from the bed, untying the du-rag that bound his long locks, and moved towards the window. Fiery rage heated his veins as he parted the beige curtains and peered down. *Who on Earth could be making all that noise?*

At the bottom floor, a large, white moving van was parked right in front of his apartment building, and it seemed a trolley-like machine was being attached to the rear of the vehicle.

He heard the annoying clanking sound again. Ah, that's the culprit, he realized. The heavy chain linking the machine to the edge of the van dragging across the front yard's cement granite ground.

Annoyed, he brushed a palm across his face as he reclined by his window and continued to observe the commotion. Who the hell was moving in, and why did the asshole feel the need to disturb the entire block of flats?

Situated at Apapa, a commercial area in Lagos, his apartment complex at *Adeshina* Estate was not a typically quiet residential area. In fact, much to the chagrin of his father and brothers who lived in upscale Banana Island, Yomi had decided to move over here to experience the real Lagos.

Since his return from London five years ago to join the family's architectural firm, he'd wanted to find his own way around Lagos. Interact with the hardworking, middle and lower class *Lagosians*. His mixed racial heritage had always made him feel different—that and the British accent he'd worked hard to shake off.

People often mocked him, discredited his authenticity whenever he tried to volunteer in community projects. Oh, if he had a Naira for every snide remark: *'you are not even a true Nigerian.' 'Oyibo man wan tell us what to do for our own country.'* And the most hurtful to him, *'you be JJC—Johnny Just Come.'* How he despised the common expression used like a weapon against a naïve foreigner.

By moving to Apapa, intermingling with *Lagosians* of diverse backgrounds, volunteering as a member of the youth community project in his neighbourhood, and sometimes abandoning his brand-new SUV to travel with public transport, he'd finally earned the respect of his neighbours and friends. He felt like a true Nigerian in every sense of the word, and he loved it, including all the upheaval living in Lagos entailed.

This city and noise pollution were as entwined as the bacon and eggs of a traditional English breakfast. One couldn't go nicely without the other. He'd grown so used to noises of blaring car horns, loud pedestrians arguing, motorcycles rearing to and fro, mob fights and loud domestic disputes, that no amount of ruckus was enough to interrupt his sleep. Or so he'd believed. Until he'd found himself awoken from his usual Saturday afternoon nap by this moving van.

"Move am forward!" one of the three men involved in attaching the monstrous machine to the back of the van yelled at the one who controlled the wheeled trolley with a lever.

"I *dey* try, but *e* too stiff," the man grumbled. Nevertheless, with an annoyed grunt, he did as he was told.

Rooted to the spot as though unable to look away, Yomi stood by the window, continuing to observe the men work. It took about two other noisy attempts before the trolley was attached to the end of the van. Their loud cheering when they'd achieved their goal put a smile on his face, and he found himself no longer annoyed but curious.

What the hell was in that van, and who on Earth was moving in? The apartment below him had been vacant for weeks after Anthony, the previous occupant—a middle-aged Italian expatriate notorious for having random women seen leaving his apartment at odd hours of the night—had left.

Yomi had been thrilled when he'd moved away. He could do without the constant reminder that he was still single and searching. But hell, who knew finding a woman, a rebel kindred spirit like him, would be so hard and take so long?

Just as he lost interest in the scene below, he noticed as a red G-wagon pulled up into the compound and parked beside the white moving van.

Seconds later, two beautiful women stepped out. But his eyes immediately settled on the tall, curvy lady sporting blond, cropped coils on her perfectly shaped head. There was something about her face, the defiant set to her jaw as she took off her sunglasses, that captivated him.

Her eyes had a shiny onyx black shade that he noticed even from his distance. And her smooth ebony skin—flawless. He'd dated all types of women with diverse physical attributes and from different races, never had been picky. However, he admittedly had a soft spot for very dark-skinned women. He couldn't explain why. But there was something about darker skin-tones that excited him.

Attention still focused on her, Yomi watched as she strode purposefully towards the van, captivated by the sway of her hips and switch of her bottom in the purple gown as she moved. Such a perfect round ass made more prominent because of her narrow waist. With full breasts also, she had an exquisite figure. One a man could get lost exploring. Not too fat, not too thin. Just right.

His groin grew heavy, and he shifted on his feet. Puzzled by his raw attraction to the stranger below, he ran his fingers through his thick locks to shake the feeling off. Then, he heard her voice ... and froze.

"Please, fellows, that piano is my most important possession. Handle with utmost care."

No mistaking who owned that voice—that sultry timbre that had captivated him from the first time he'd heard it. The only soundtrack to his most erotic dreams. The voice he'd inexplicably fallen in love with— Sasha.

CHAPTER THREE

"Please be gentle ... please ..."

Emem's stomach tightened as she watched her beloved piano being transferred from the back of the van onto a large trolley, which the hired movers had assured her would ensure nothing happened to it.

"Madam, don't worry *nau*. We told you we know what we are doing," grunted the burly man who had stepped into the back of the van, his forehead furrowed in annoyance. "That's what this machine is for, to roll the piano into the building."

"Thank you ... thank you."

She sighed, although still worried. She'd had all her other furniture moved in last week while she stayed with Natalie, who shared a flat with her sister on the other end of town. But this piece? It was most important of all. Truth be told, everything else could be blasted to smithereens. But her piano was beyond precious.

Although they had asked her to stay with them, Emem wanted her own flat. And this was the best she could afford to rent. A two-bedroom, self-contained apartment in a noisy, poorly maintained estate. A huge downgrade from the upscale area where she'd stayed. So, she wanted her only valued possession delivered safely here. A reminder of the comfortable life she had abandoned before moving to Lagos to struggle with a man who didn't even love her.

"Calm down, Emem. You're always so type A. You paid these men, let them do their jobs."

Natalie's soft voice of reason interrupted her thoughts, bringing some tranquillity to her heightened senses.

She really needed to relax. This was her second time moving this piano. And the anxiety was still the same. She remembered when she'd had to move it from Port Harcourt to Lagos. She'd been unable to sleep, worried that the only legacy she had from her grandmother would be damaged or lost. She wouldn't be able to bear it if that happened. But she had to let go and trust the professionals.

She nodded, stepping back.

"Okay," she whispered, glad that her best friend was here.

She and Natalie had met on a plane en route from Port Harcourt to Lagos five years ago. Then, Natalie had been relocating for a new job, and she, on the other hand, had been relocating for a man. Ironic that now, Natalie was the one in a loving relationship whereas she'd become single.

A sudden wave of sadness hit her. As though Natalie sensed it, she draped an arm around her shoulders.

"Chill, girl. Everything will be okay," she said, a reassuring lilt in her voice. "That man isn't worth your grief."

Emem's throat constricted, a jolt of regret stabbing her chest.

"Thanks, dear," she croaked, suddenly fighting tears. "I know."

It had to be all right. She had to move past this. Be strong. Starting with getting herself settled into her first apartment alone. Although nervous about the prospect of living on her own for the first time, she believed that's what she needed to finally get over

Ejike. To focus on herself, for once, without having to care for or think about anyone else.

Silently, she stood watching as the three hired movers successfully transferred the piano onto the trolley. She smiled when they shouted their satisfaction.

"I told you, madam! We know what we are doing," the burly man who appeared to be the leader of the team erupted, pride brimming in his eyes.

Emem chuckled. "Yes, sir. You did, indeed."

A slow warmth swept over her. Maybe everything would turn out okay. *Maybe I'll finally move past this.*

Just as the comforting thought entered her mind, a man emerged from the opened front door.

No. A god. Almost too stunning for words. Tall, with broad shoulders, smooth, golden skin, too light for her usual taste, but the complexion on him enhanced rather than deterred from his good looks. With a long nose and fine facial features, he looked biracial, posh, and out of place in a local area like this.

As he strutted towards them, she found herself instinctively holding her breath, everyone fading away from her line of vision as her gaze narrowed on him. Such a knockout. The long, jet-black dreadlocks with blond highlights hanging from his head down to his shoulders reminded her of Ziggy Marley. He was dressed in a pair of ripped blue jeans and a black tank top, which brought attention to strong, muscular arms showcasing large Chinese calligraphy tattoos on each side.

Embarrassed to be staring at his arms, she jumped her gaze back to his face, and heat burned her cheeks at the arrogant glint in his eyes. He obviously knew how stunning he was, and probably got this same reaction from women.

A quick side glance at Natalie's rigid posture told of her own awestruck response to the man's beauty.

"Welcome to our block of flats, beautiful ladies," he said, standing right in front of them, legs akimbo. Confident. Rugged.

Both still speechless, they didn't respond. And he didn't seem to be bothered by their silence. He swept his gaze to the movers who had begun pushing the trolley towards the front entrance, and then back at them.

He cast a quick glance at Natalie before he focused his attention on her. His lips parted in a slow grin, exposing white teeth and gorgeous bilateral dimples.

"I'm Yomi Oladipo, and I live upstairs in Apartment Eight," he said, an arrogant drawl in his voice as he offered her his hand.

Emem ignored it, but Natalie reached out and shook it vigorously, allowing her fingers to linger for moments.

"I'm Natalie," she gushed, grinning from molar to molar.

He smiled at Natalie, his dimples making another stunning appearance.

"Hello, Natalie. I can't believe how lucky I am to have a beautiful lady like you moving into this building," he drawled, a slight British accent in his intonation.

Natalie blushed, and Emem felt like slapping her across the face. *You have a man, girl*, she thought bitingly, not wanting to analyse the annoyance dripping through her at seeing her friend flirting with this stranger.

"I'm not moving in." Natalie sounded disappointed. "I'm helping my friend, Emem, move in."

His gaze moved back to her, and Emem's chest spasmed.

"Emem ... a lovely name for a beauty," he said, shoving both hands into his jeans pockets, as though accepting her refusal to shake.

Emem fought back the desire to roll her eyes at his cheesy lines. A fuck boy. A young fuck boy who didn't think twice about making a pass at older women. Nope. Not interested. No matter how handsome, she was not in the mood for this.

"Can I help you move in, too, Emem?" he asked, his tone dripping with honey.

"No, thank you. We are fine," she answered curtly.

"Oh, my ... yes!" Natalie said at the same time in a shrill voice.

The man's gaze jumped to Natalie and then settled back on her. His thick, perfectly carved eyebrow arched.

"One Yes and one No," he drawled, seemingly unfazed by her rudeness. "Which is it, ladies?"

Emem shook her head. She really had no time for this young dreadlocked fuck boy. She had stuff to do. "Thanks, Mister, but I'm good."

She threw an exasperated glance at her friend who still appeared spellbound by the stranger.

"Natalie, *abeg*, let's go and bring the rest of my stuff from the car."

Sucking her teeth, Emem walked around the man, aware she was being rude but not caring. She needed to nip this right in the bud. He lived in the apartment just above hers, and she didn't want him becoming too friendly.

The move to this place was for her to heal and regain her focus. Not to have to deal with an overtly cocky neighbour knocking on her door whenever he felt like it, thinking he could get lucky.

Natalie flashed an apologetic smile at the man before she followed.

"*Haba*, Emem, he's only trying to help," her friend whispered as she walked closely beside her.

"And you were only trying to ogle him to death."

"Don't blame me. He's hot."

"And you have a man."

"So?" Natalie's eyebrow curved upwards. "I am in a relationship. Not blind. And it's harmless flirting. You should try that sometimes. I noticed your reaction to him, too, you know."

Emem harrumphed in response.

Fighting back the desire to glance back at the man, she strutted towards her friend's car and opened the boot. She reached for her suitcase and lifted it with a grunt.

"I'm not interested. I don't need all that rubbish, *mbok*," she said as she set it on the ground and adjusted the handle. "From helping me move in, he'll think I owe him and that he can just knock on my door whenever he wants."

"*Haba*! So what if he does? Is that the worst thing in the world?"

"Yes. I'm here to get myself back together. Work on me, for once. I'm in no mood for fuck boys."

"And you know he's a fuck boy from meeting him the first time, how?" Natalie twisted her lips as she spoke.

"Come on, Natalie ... look at him." She pivoted her head in his direction. Natalie also turned her attention towards the apartment entrance.

He stood beside the moving van, feet spread apart and hands in his pockets. He was speaking to two of the movers who appeared to be working on getting the trolley back into the van.

They both roared with laughter at what he said, and he laughed, too, his own laughter pleasantly distinguishable to her ears. A rich, deep sound. Her abdominal muscles contracted. Apparently, her rudeness hadn't spoilt his mood.

"That's the problem with you—jumping to conclusions too quickly. He seems like a friendly sort of neighbour," Natalie mumbled, snagging back her attention. "And even if he is a fuck boy, so what? You may not even be his type. Did he *toast* you? He could have been interested in me. Or neither of us."

Emem paused. That was true. The man hadn't come onto her. He'd actually addressed them both. Except ... she glanced at him again, and their eyes met and held. Her heart jumped, and blood rushed to her head. The intensity reflected in his dark eyes made her feel dizzy.

Nope, he hadn't come onto her. But there was something in his eyes when he'd looked at her earlier that had made her feel exposed. As soon as he'd stepped out of the house, he'd narrowed his attention on her as if he knew her, recognised her. Strange, but she'd felt like he knew her deepest secrets.

Flustered, she looked away. But not before she noticed the slow grin that spread across his remarkably handsome face, and the spark of excitement that registered in his eyes. She had awakened something in him. A connection—maybe. Lust—most likely. Whatever it was, it unnerved her.

Shaking her head to clear her mind from those ridiculous thoughts, she slammed the boot shut.

"You're right, Natalie. I was rude. I'll apologise to him later," she said.

"Good," Natalie said, nodding. "You don't want to start alienating your neighbours. This is Lagos. You need supportive neighbours."

She agreed with her friend. No need antagonising a neighbour. This was a rough neighbourhood, and she needed to ensure she had friends where she lived. Not enemies.

Emem cast her attention back to the front entrance. The man was no longer there. Only the movers remained by the van, sharing their earnings amongst themselves.

A regretful sigh escaped her lips. She hadn't meant to lash out at him. In fact, she'd been more annoyed at herself than at him. Her attraction to him confused and irritated her. Having allowed her infatuation with Ejike to lead her down a path where she'd lost her own identity, she never wanted to feel that kind of attraction to any man ever again.

However, that didn't give her the right to be rude to him or anyone, for that matter. She needed to get her head right. This angry person wasn't her at all.

"I'll apologise to him later," she said again.

Natalie nodded. "Okay, then, let's get you settled in now that your beloved piano is safely inside," she said, rolling her eyes.

They both chuckled.

CHAPTER FOUR

"Segun, you're in charge of pitching this model to the Imo State governor," announced Yomi's father.

Yomi heard Chief Dele Oladipo's decision issued from the other end of the oval-shaped conference table, but he had to be hearing things. Seated beside his brothers, Segun and Kunle, he blew out a harsh gasp of shock.

This was the last thing he'd expected at the scheduled Monday morning meeting to discuss the proposed recreational centre for Imo State. Oladipo and Sons Architectural Firm was amongst the three firms bidding for the contract, and he'd worked his butt off on the project.

"What?" he erupted. He felt like a ten-ton lorry had just run over his heart. "I was the one who took the lead on this. The one who spent sleepless nights going over the structures repeatedly until it ended up exactly the way we'd envisioned it."

He pointed at the construction prototype set in the centre of the conference table as he spoke, unable to believe that after all the hard work he had put into this, his father was willing to sidestep him and give the credit to his older brother. Just like he'd always done. It was as though he continually wanted to make it clear that Segun, his first son from his late first wife, was the favourite of his three children.

Little things he did and said over the years since they were children implied this, but he continually denied this accusation every time confronted about it. And here he was, doing it again.

"I did all the bloody work," Yomi reiterated, an angry flush burning his cheeks.

His father sighed. "I know, son, and it's excellent work." He hesitated, blew out a short breath. "But I can't send you to present it."

"Why the hell not? You didn't send me for the other four projects, either." He clenched his jaw. "I tried to understand then, but I figured I wasn't the main architect for those projects. But this right here ..." He thrust his index finger at the model again. "This is my goddamned baby. I am the one who should give the presentation."

"Listen, Yomi, can we talk about this another time?" asked his father, his even tone irritating him further. "We still have other agenda items to discuss."

"No!" he barked. "I get the distinct feeling you don't believe in me ... don't trust me."

"It's not that, son."

"Why the hell can't I be the one to present this?"

"Yomi, this is not the place—"

"Just tell me I'm not good enough," he interjected, his voice hoarse as his irritation grew. "I know you are ashamed that I graduated with a third class ... I'm dyslexic. Not dumb."

"Drop this now, Yomi. I never said you were dumb." His father's eyes flashed.

"So why can't I present this to the governor?"

Silence. The tense atmosphere seemed to suck all the air out of the moderate-sized conference room as father and son glared at each other.

Grinding his jaw, Yomi pinned his father with a challenging gaze, awaiting his response, uncaring that his two brothers shifted in their seats uncomfortably, uneasiness slicing through the room.

"Dad, maybe we should let Yomi take the lead this time." This came from Segun. "It is his work, after all."

"I know," his father said, turning to Segun. "I have my reasons, and—"

"Care to share?" Yomi interrupted.

"Okay, Yomi," his father erupted. "You are brilliant. An amazing architect. But ..."

His stomach clenched, dread for the next words causing cold sweat to prickle the skin of his back. Did his father consider him incompetent, unable to do a good job securing this contract? Wasn't he good enough?

"But, your dreadlocks ..." A loud sigh erupted from his father. "I mean ... why don't you cut that rag from your head, eh? It makes you appear unserious, and I can't take the chance of losing this contract because of your appearance."

"My dreadlocks?" Yomi choked out, flabbergasted.

Of all the things he had expected to hear, this wasn't close. He almost felt relieved. It had nothing to do with his abilities. Just his appearance.

Living in Nigeria for the past five years and even a few times while living in England, his locks had been a source of discrimination from people in the corporate world. He'd grown used to being told that they made him look uncivilised, unruly. In fact, one of his lecturers in university back in England, a black man, had suggested that he needed to cut his hair before he could be taken seriously in the architectural business.

So, this wasn't new to him. He'd always been prepared for this comment, although he felt a bit taken aback that his own father, who had only teased him lightly about his locks, had used it as a reason to deny him an opportunity.

"Yes, son." His father's words brought his mind back. "This is Nigeria, not England. The governor may be put off by how you look and not give us the contract simply because of that."

Yomi ran his fingers through his neatly packed locks and burst into laughter. As if infected by his amusement, his brothers, including his father, joined in, laughing loudly for moments until the room became quiet again.

"Well, I am sorry to hear that," he said. "I will never cut the so-called *rag* from my head. It's my identity as a black man. I am proud of it. And if other people with self-hate can't accept my locks, they should kiss my ass."

"Language ..." his father warned.

"I don't give a f—" He sucked in a calming breath. "I don't care. If that's the case, let Segun present it."

"I hope you understand this isn't about your abilities—" his father began.

"I don't understand squat, Dad," Yomi cut in. "I'll never understand why some Africans are ashamed of their own heritage. Locks used to be a source of cultural pride before others told us they made us look unruly and uncivilised—called them *dreadlocks*." He made air quotes with his fingers. "There is nothing dreadful about leaving my hair in its natural state."

Encouraged by the approving nods from his brothers, he continued. "We as a continent need to gain back our self-pride and stop trying so hard to be accepted by others."

Loud applause followed his declaration. Yomi grinned as he settled back in his seat.

"Great speech, Yomi," his father said, twisting his lips. "But this is a three-hundred-million Naira contract we hope to get, and not everyone is as open-minded as you are. So, for now, let Segun be the one to present the work, okay?"

Yomi hesitated for seconds, glanced at his brother whose eyes reflected empathy, and nodded.

The meeting lasted another hour, and by the time it was over, he felt drained.

Seated at his desk in his office on the third floor overlooking the high streets, he peered at the computer in front of him, flicking through digital images of portrait paintings.

He paused at one in particular and sucked his teeth.

"Excellent work," he murmured. "Real talent."

Shifting his gaze to the top of the screen, he located the name of the artist. Ehi Osunde. Seventeen years old.

Wow. He was amazed at the efficient blending of colours that produced the striking picture of a woman holding a bowl of tropical fruits in her hands. Even the reflection of hope in her eyes had been brilliantly captured by the young artist.

"You've definitely qualified for the final round, Ehi," he whispered as he dragged the image with his desktop mouse and moved it to the Finalists' folder.

As one of the three volunteer judges for a local art competition organised by the youth association of his neighbourhood, he had to hand in the final scores of watercolour paintings by the participants in a week.

He needed to go through all the images before the weekend. Although now narrowed down to thirty contestants, he still had to come up with the final ten in the lot.

Yomi rubbed his fingers over his eyes and stretched his arms above his head, yawning.

"Bloody tired," he muttered to himself.

Last night, he had pushed aside the painting competition and stayed awake, putting the finishing touches to the architectural model. He'd retreated to bed in the early hours of the morning only when he'd felt satisfied.

Now, he had time to devote to the contest, but he also wanted to go back home and catch up on sleep. At least, he still had a few days before he needed to turn the final scores in. A lazy evening in bed was all he needed, and he would be rejuvenated.

Resolving to ensure he did just that, he left the office as soon as he finished all his outstanding paperwork. Satisfied with the complete presentation he'd put together, he handed them to his brother and drove home.

Luckily, the traffic was light, and he arrived within forty minutes. A miracle, considering it usually took him almost two hours to get home every day. The universe certainly agreed that he needed some rest.

After parking at his designated spot inside the compound, he angled his head towards the corner purposefully, and his heart skipped a beat. Sasha was home. Her small black Honda was in its usual parking spot.

Pulse hammering as he walked past her front door on his way to the staircase, Yomi wondered if he should just knock on her door and say hello. He wanted to clear the air between them, talk to her. It had been one week since she'd moved in, and he hadn't seen her. Not even once. A major disappointment.

To be honest with himself, he usually lingered briefly by her door on his way in and out of the building, fighting the compulsion to knock, or even hoping she would suddenly emerge from her house and bump into him. But she seemed a reclusive sort. Which surprised him.

From years of listening to her on the radio, he'd imagined her to be different. Younger ... boisterous, social. He suspected she was in her mid-thirties.

Although from the flawlessness of her skin and the youthful glow of her face, she could pass for a younger woman, her eyes gave her age away. A subtle maturity shone in them. And something else. Wariness.

She appeared fed-up. Like she didn't want to be bothered by people. She'd told him just that—rudely—when he had tried to help her move in. But her rudeness hadn't repulsed him. Instead, it had made him curious. Strangely made him even more turned on. Yes. He wanted to get to know Sasha better.

Pestering her won't help your cause, he thought, shaking his head. It was best to take things slowly. She lived below his apartment. He would surely bump into her at some point. Maybe then, he would make his move. No need to rush. He was a patient man.

Whistling, he climbed the first flight of stairs. Just as he reached the bottom of the second set of stairs leading to his apartment, he halted dead in his tracks.

In front of his door stood Sasha, knuckles poised to knock.

Blood rushed to his head, and his chest muscles spasmed, knocking his breath away.

"Sasha?" he erupted before he could stop himself.

She spun around, eyes wide in shock, eyebrows raised in question.

"How do you …" She broke off. "That's my radio name … how do you know it?"

Yomi's lips slanted into a half-smile, his heart thudding rapidly in his chest, unbelievably happy to see her standing by his front door. Sooner than he'd expected. But a welcome surprise. She'd come to seek him out.

"I've listened to *Late Nights with Sasha* every Friday for the past five years," he said, resuming his climb up the stairs. "Your voice is quite memorable."

Soothing, yet husky. A pleasant sound that floats forever in my head, he wanted to add, but held his tongue. He rested his frame against the wall when he got to her.

"You're here to see me?" he asked instead, lips still slanted in a smile.

CHAPTER FIVE

The way her heart was beating so fast, Emem felt it would rupture her ribcage. This stunning man knew her as Sasha, had been listening to her talk about sex and whatnot on the radio.

Oh, God. This had never happened to her. She'd never met anyone who had recognised her from her radio show. Not once.

Completely anonymous, she'd never shown her face to the public, and for years, had coasted in the bliss of anonymity, saying whatever she pleased on the show. Her alter ego, Sasha, was as bold and reckless as she'd never let herself be.

To think that someone recognised her, had listened to her, and could now put a face to her uncensored sex and relationship talk over the radio made her body flood with heat.

"Is everything okay?"

His worried question brought her mind back.

"Y—Yes," she replied. "I'm … I'm just shocked. I've been anonymous for years."

He let out a low chuckle. The sound sent a wave of awareness down her body.

"Well … not to me." He regarded her with an amused glint in his eyes. "I'm a huge fan of your radio show."

Heat burned Emem's cheeks as she stood there flustered by the intensity of his gaze. He had a way of looking at her like he knew all her secrets.

She suddenly remembered how he'd made her feel the first time they'd met. The sensation that he'd recognised or had met her before. Now, she knew why. He somewhat knew a little about her, having spent years listening to all her brazen radio talk.

Her stomach roiled as she remembered last Friday's show when she had given a caller advice about sexual positions to try during pregnancy. Oh, Lord, all the things she'd said. Had he listened? What did he think about that?

"I see you have something for me, I hope?"

His deep voice crashed through her thoughts.

Emem glanced down at the covered tray in her hands and twisted her lips nervously.

"Oh, yes. I came to apologise for my rudeness last week," she said, raising her gaze to his again. "I was just having a bad day and didn't mean to take it out on you."

"No worries at all. I figured as much," he said.

"I baked a cake for you—" She lifted the dome covering the tray. "Chocolate cake. I hope you're not allergic to that, and nuts."

"Ah, I love chocolate," he murmured, his eyes moving leisurely from the treat and over her face like a slow caress. "Especially dark chocolate. No allergies. Only eager taste buds."

Warmth flooded her entire being at the suggestiveness of his tone. What a flirt. A handsome flirt. He looked virile in a charcoal black suit that fit his muscular frame like it was made for him. His dreadlocks were packed away from his face, emphasising a strong jaw covered in a slight stubble, and chiselled facial features.

And by God, he smelled heavenly. Even the aroma of chocolate icing from the cake couldn't drown out the scent of his cologne as it floated through her nostrils. Sandalwood, citrus, and a mixture of something else that made her want to bury her face in his neck and get lost in the tantalising fragrance of maleness he exuded.

Emem shook her head, trying to clear her mind from this nonsense. *He is a child, for goodness' sake.* She wondered how old—he looked like an eighteen-year-old boy. Okay, not a boy. There was nothing juvenile about the way his eyes roamed over her body with confidence. He looked a bit older than a teenager. Maybe in his early twenties. But still too young. *Forget it, girl. You're almost forty.*

"Okay, then." She extended the offering to him, wanting to rush away from there and make sense of the wayward beating of her heart and the carnal response this man's mere presence produced within her. "Here's your cake. And once again, sorry for my rudeness. It won't happen again."

He eyed the contents of her hands but didn't make any move to take what she offered.

"Well, thanks. But I won't accept until you come in for a while and have some tea. We'll share the cake," he said, tiny smile lines puckering the corner of his dark eyes as he spoke.

"No, I don't want to be a bother. I just wanted to—"

"Apologise and give me some homemade chocolate cake," he cut in. "I know. And I will accept the kind-hearted gesture only on the condition that you come in and share it with me."

Silence. She looked around, suddenly worried. She didn't know this man. He could be a rapist or murderer. Lagos wasn't a place where you entered the homes of strangers without caution.

"Don't worry, I live in this building with you, so you are safe."

She hesitated still.

His face stretched into a charming smile. "Do you have your phone with you?"

She nodded, chewing her lower lip, unsure where he was going with this.

"Good. Text your friend ... Natalie. Tell her you just walked into my apartment, and ask her to ring you if you don't call her in thirty minutes."

Emem couldn't help the grin that spread across her lips. His suggestion seemed reasonable enough. Handing him the small tray, she retrieved her phone from her denim pocket and did just that.

Almost immediately, her phone chimed back with a shocked emoji and an eggplant emoji text message lighting the screen. She shook her head. Natalie was never serious. Everything revolved around sex with her.

"A naughty text?" Yomi asked, amusement dancing in his eyes.

She nodded in response. "My friend is a nut case."

He laughed.

"We need people like that in our lives," he said, fishing out a bunch of keys from his pocket and then opening the door.

Excited and nervous at the same time, she followed him inside his apartment. Her eyes widened.

"Nice," she whispered, taking in the modern decor of the room.

Pristine cream-coloured leather furniture arranged artistically in the large sitting room faced a massive flat screen television anchored to the beige walls. Five large landscape paintings hung strategically at the corners of the room gave a serene vibe to the space.

"You do like the colour white," she teased. "This looks like a picture from a real-estate magazine. Everything bright and spotless."

He grinned as he strode farther in, carrying the tray towards the adjacent room which she assumed to be the kitchen.

"Make yourself comfortable," he said, disappearing inside.

"I feel like I can't with all the immaculate furnishing around me. I'm afraid to stain anything."

She heard his rich laughter, the sound deep and distracting.

"Oh, come on," he called from the kitchen. "It's not even like that."

"It is so. Everything in here looks spotless and arranged by a neat freak."

"Okay, I admit it. I have a thing for order. I get nervous when things aren't placed exactly like I want them. And yes. I prefer white furniture. That way, it's easy to spot something messy."

"Oh, a bit of OCD going on?"

"Maybe. But I think it's just a way to have some control over things."

She heard the sound of a kettle boiling water and halted her descent into the seat directly opposite the television.

"You need me to help?" she asked.

"No, I'm fine," he said, his voice closer than seconds before.

She turned to find him back in the sitting room with two saucers in his hands. He had taken off his suit jacket and tie, showcasing firm arm muscles bulging through the white shirt he wore. Her heart fluttered as she sank into the plush leather. He truly had an impeccable build. Athletic, but not too buff.

"Here's your slice," he said, handing her one. "Looks delicious, and I can't wait to dig in."

"Thanks. I enjoy baking. Helps me relax. I hope you like it."

He lowered the saucer in his hand on a small coffee table in front of him. "I'm sure I will. Like I said, I love anything made with chocolate."

There was a sultry drawl in his tone as he said that, drawing an unwanted but unstoppable heated response within her, tightening the bud between her thighs. She crossed one leg over the other hastily to stifle the sudden arousal flooding her nether region.

His eyes followed her movement and trailed up leisurely back to hers. As though aware of her plight, his mouth lifted into a cocky grin. Moments of silence ticked by, her heart jackhammering in her chest.

How could this young man make her feel like an inexperienced teenager with just his gaze? She felt completely foolish for her response to him, and yet, she couldn't control it. What the hell was happening to her? Mid-life crisis?

A loud chime emanated from the kitchen, crashing through her musings. She started, eyes widening.

"The kettle. It's five years old and noisy as hell," he explained, the corner of his lips tilting into a small smile. "Tea or coffee?"

"Tea, please."

"Sugar? Milk?"

She raised a brow in amusement. "Do you know any Nigerian that drinks tea without milk and sugar?"

He erupted into laughter, and she watched in fascination as his chest muscles rippled as he roared unabashedly.

"Actually, no," he said, still chuckling. "First thing I learnt when I returned from England. Never make tea without milk and sugar for a Nigerian. And every warm beverage is called tea. Including coffee and chocolate drinks."

"True. True," she affirmed. "Don't forget to add that every chocolate drink is called Milo, irrespective of the brand."

"Yes! Oh, God, I love this country," he declared, his eyes twinkling.

She couldn't help but smile, unexpectedly thrilled at the carefree banter between them.

"Ah ... means you're still a JJC. Only non-Nigerians or British Nigerians like yourself can make that comment."

He stiffened, and his jaw muscles tightened.

"I'm sorry. Did I say something wrong?"

She held his gaze and noticed a brief flash in his eyes. Sadness? Regret? Why? It was so fleeting that she could have imagined it.

"No, it's nothing ..."

"It's something all right. Tell me. I'm sorry if—"

"JJC. I hate being called that."

"Oh, I didn't mean to ... I didn't know."

"No worries. It's my issue, not yours. You did nothing wrong."

"Well, I'm sorry ...." She paused, stroking her finger idly over the leather couch's armrest. "Mind if I ask why?"

"Not at all. I'll tell you. But first, let me get the tea ..." A mischievous smile curved his lips, his face once again relaxed into a carefree expression. "... with plenty of milk and sugar."

"Thanks," she said, happy to see him relaxed again, yet inexplicably curious about this young handsome man in front of her. "But just a cube of sugar will do."

"Okay." He chuckled as he strolled back into the kitchen.

CHAPTER SIX

Yomi scooped a slice of the cake with his fork and lifted it to his mouth.

"Hmm, nice," he murmured as the succulent chocolate dessert melted on his tongue, igniting his palate's sensory nerves. "Perfect."

He took another forkful and savoured the taste once again.

"Thank you," she muttered, her smile shy.

Oh, how that shy smile enticed him unbearably at the moment. He sat across from her, torn between relishing the delicious treat on his plate and eliminating the distance between them for a taste of her full lips.

He couldn't explain his intense attraction to her. It felt primal, beyond his control, which was crazy really, because he didn't believe in that sort of thing.

Yes, she was beautiful, but not the most beautiful woman he'd seen. And honestly, she didn't seem like what he'd expected her to be from listening to her show. This Sasha before him was demure, and not at all like the uninhibited one he'd listened to for years.

Instead of that dampening his enthusiasm, it aroused his interests even more—the contradiction, the complexity of who she was. Emem, who could also be Sasha when she decided to be. He wanted to know every facet of her personality. And he intended to.

"So ... the JJC story. I'm dying to hear it," she said, her husky voice breaking through his thoughts.

He watched as she took a sip of her tea. Her delicate fingers crowned with finely manicured nails clutched the mug handle in an almost sensual way that made him want them around his—

The sudden tightening of his groin jarred him back to reality. He redirected his focus to her comment.

"Oh, that," he said. "The most embarrassing and humiliating story about my return to Lagos."

"Now, I'm curious."

She sat forward, forehead creased up, and gaze pinned on him. Her interest was almost palpable. Although he loathed telling this story, for strange reasons, it felt right sharing it with her.

"When I decided to move back to Nigeria, I thought I had it all figured out. As the last of three sons, I'd always felt overlooked, like I was not as capable as my brothers, wasn't good enough." Yomi reclined in his seat, took a sip of his hot tea, and continued. "I mean, my brothers keep trying to assure me that isn't the case, but I'd always felt insecure, like I was in their shadow."

Her eyebrows angled together in question.

"You see, they both graduated first class in architecture with honours, and both attained Distinction in their Master's degrees in estate management before joining the family architectural firm—the only thing my father cares about. Whereas I struggled to even complete uni with a third class," he explained.

"Degree classifications don't mean a lot in this country, anyway," she said, giving him an understanding smile. "I heard that Wole Soyinka, one of the best poets and writers of all time, got a third class. I'm sure you worked hard. And that's all that matters."

"Oh, I did. I worked my ass off in spite of my limitations."

"Limitations?" Her forehead crinkled.

He paused, suddenly worried about revealing his shortcomings to her. She seemed like an intellectual and witty sort who may not understand his academic challenges. Would she think less of him?

"I'm dyslexic," he admitted, deciding to be upfront. "I find it difficult to read, write, or spell. I need to re-read things repeatedly before I can understand or recall the details."

Stomach coiled into a tight knot, he searched her face, expecting to see repulsion. Or worse ... pity. Odd, but she didn't even seem startled. Only interest shone from her beautiful dark eyes. Simply like someone keen to hear his tale.

He blew out a relieved breath. Her lack of response made him feel better. As if it didn't change anything between them. Certainly, not the usual reaction he got when he told people about his learning disability. The suddenly shuttered look, the slight lean backward, the quick exit—making him feel different, inadequate. Until now. Until Sasha.

A vague warmth settled in his chest, and his cheeks grew hot. Her presence here felt right, comforting. He had exposed his vulnerability to her, but it wasn't weird at all. Rather, he wanted to tell her more.

"So, when it was time to move back to join the firm, I wanted to do it myself. Not ask for help," he went on, crossing his legs at the ankles. "I told my brothers and father that I would do it all on my own. If I could live alone in the off-campus university flat in Kent, I could certainly fend for myself in Lagos."

Her lips slanted into a smile.

"Ha! Even people born and raised in Lagos are not that confident." She shook her head. "I remember when I moved here from Port Harcourt. Everyone kept warning me about life here. It felt like I was moving to

Hell." She released a snort of laughter. "That's exactly how people make you feel about this city. But I have really come to love the chaos. I don't think I could live anywhere else in this country. You need to explore more of Nigeria. Abuja, Jos, Calabar—my favourite city."

"Your hometown?"

"No, close though. I'm from Akwa Ibom." she answered, giving him another shy smile.

He sensed her reluctance to talk about herself. Although he wanted to continue to explore her background, he decided to continue with his story instead. There would be lots of time to get to know her better. He would make sure of that.

"I searched for a real-estate agent online who had a beautifully designed block of flats showcased in a convincing website. According to the advertisement, they were two-bedroom apartments located in a gated estate in Victoria Island. Quite lovely houses and at ridiculously affordable prices for such a classy location."

"Almost too good to be true," she huffed.

"Exactly," he said, shaking his head. "But I was so excited that I'd discovered this treasure by myself, without the help of my family. Finally, I could tell them I did something on my own. So, I called the agent from London, and after a few repeated phone calls, borrowed money from the bank, and transferred ten thousand pounds, a percentage of the down payment for purchase."

He let out a self-deprecating laugh. "I mean, he sounded so educated on the phone, so helpful. There was even a website with about thirty rave reviews. I never once suspected it was all a scam."

"Oh, how horrid!" she gasped. "People are just horrible."

"I know!" he agreed, renewed embarrassment burning his face. "You can imagine how humiliated I felt when I arrived and found there weren't any houses like that. It was all a made-up website with fake pictures from the Internet. The buildings were not even from Nigeria but from Gabon."

"Lord, I hope you informed the police."

"Oh, I rushed over to the police station as soon as I discovered this, enraged and full of righteous indignation." He raked his palm over his face, remembering the frustration of sitting in the cramped and shabby police station beside his brothers as they waited for hours before someone attended to them. "That was where I heard the term JJC for the first time used by the officers as they repeatedly mocked me. They kept asking, 'How can you be so foolish?', and saying, 'These foreigners are so stupid' with such pleasure, taking delight in my misfortune."

"That's awful," she muttered. Her eyes narrowed to annoyed slits. "They are supposed to help, not laugh at a victim."

"They didn't help at all. I lost all that money. Five years later, that conman has still not been arrested."

He clenched his jaw. That wasn't the worse part to him. It was the fact that, once again, he'd not read between the lines, not done proper research, and had acted immaturely. Although his father and brothers had refrained from pointing that out, he saw the disappointment in their eyes as they sorted him out with accommodation.

"Since then, being called JJC makes my stomach churn, reminds me of how gullible I'd been."

"Awww ... don't beat yourself up. Everyone in this country has one or two stories about being scammed. It has nothing to do with being a foreigner."

"That's the thing. I don't want to be seen as a foreigner. I'm half Nigerian, half English. I regret that my father didn't expose me much to his side of my heritage. I was born and raised in England, and rarely returned for holidays. I hated that feeling of being different when I moved back to Nigeria. I hated my accent, that I can't speak or understand Yoruba. I felt like a JJC, and that's why it hurt. Because it was somewhat true. I wanted to change that. Needed to."

He was startled by his own vehemence. He'd never shared this with anyone.

"Is that why you live in this horrible part of town?"

Her tone had a teasing ring to it, perhaps an attempt to lighten the mood.

He gave her a smile. "Yes. My family is horrified that I live here. They say the neighbourhood is a bit rougher than what I'm used to. Although I agree, I've enjoyed experiencing the hustle of living like a real Nigerian. I've grown so much. At least now, nobody can call me a JJC. It's the best decision I've made."

The fact that Sasha, the woman with the voice that had captivated him from the first time he'd heard it, now lived in the same building, made that feeling even all the more satisfying.

A moment of silence ensued. He watched as she lifted a forkful of cake to her lips, his attention drawn to their succulent fullness. As though sensing his perusal, her gaze jumped to his and held.

His pulse began pounding in his ears. This was it. The moment to ask her out. He had her full attention now.

"Sasha..." he began.

"Emem," she interjected. "Please call me Emem."

"Emem, I would like to take you out on a date, maybe dinner."

Silence. The diameter of her eyes increased, a soft gasp escaping her parted lips.

"I'm thirty-eight years old," she sputtered.

He lifted a brow, puzzled. "So?"

"Well, I'm way older than you."

He curved his lips into a half-smile. "And how old do you think I am?"

She hesitated, fidgeted with the fork in her hand, placed it on the saucer she held, and lowered it to the tea table in front of her.

"Early twenties?" she answered, a tentative lilt in her voice.

"Twenty-nine."

"Still too young to be asking me out. Surely, you have younger girlfriends. I'm almost ten years older than you."

"Nope. I'm single. And what has age got to do with the attraction we feel for each other?"

"Attraction we feel? Speak for yourself. I don't have any feelings for you other than friendliness."

"So, if I walk over, pull you into my arms, and kiss you right now, you won't feel anything?" he challenged. "Your heart won't beat faster? Your body won't tremble?"

Her mouth parted into a wide 'O'.

Emem's expression of shock sent a shiver of excitement down his spine. He wanted to test his theory so badly.

"No! And you will do no such thing," she shrieked.

"Then, say yes. This Saturday, we could go to a nice restaurant. I can get tickets to watch a play at the national theatre afterwards."

A spark of interest lit her eyes for seconds before she shook her head. "I don't think it's wise. We shouldn't ..."

"Why not? It would only be a date, a more intimate opportunity to get to know each other better. I want to know more about you."

Her breath hitched, as though surprised at his audacity. She remained silent, gaping at him, breath coming out in shallow spurts.

Eager to persuade her, he waded into the silence. "You are a stunning, smart, and sexy woman. I'm a warm-blooded man who is interested in you. And I sense your interest in me." He ignored her head-shake of denial. "What's the big deal?"

She chewed her lower lip for seconds, making her even more irresistible to him. She opened her mouth to respond, but a loud ringing sound stopped her. She pulled out the phone from her pocket, glanced at the screen, and then answered.

"I'm fine, Natalie. Sorry, I should have called. Was a little distracted." Her fingers trembled slightly as she held the mobile device against her cheek. "No, not that kind of distraction, girl." She glanced his way, a tell-tale embarrassed glint in her eyes. "I'm hanging up. Thanks, sweetie. Speak to you soon."

Silence followed the termination of her phone call. He looked intently at her, waiting for her response.

"I just got out of a relationship," she muttered finally, rising to her feet. "I'm not interested in dating anyone for now."

Her answer made his heart sink, like he'd been punched in the gut. For the first time ever, a woman turning him down felt like a major setback. Usually carefree about such things, he took rejection well, sometimes even jovially.

However, with Emem, he couldn't just let go. From the first time he'd heard her voice and then when he'd seen her, there'd been an immediate surge of relief within. As though he'd finally found what he'd been searching for all his life. His soulmate. Corny—he knew, but he couldn't help the way he felt.

Indeed, he would keep trying to win her trust, persuade her to let her guard down and let him in. Because of her recent split, convincing her would be much more challenging. But he was up to the task. He'd just have to be patient. Move with deliberate caution.

Her husky voice interrupted his musings.

"Thanks for a pleasant evening. And for tea," she said, walking towards the door.

He followed her, trying not to show his disappointment. "You're welcome. And thanks for the lovely cake."

She flashed him a small smile, turned, and reached for the door knob. Impulsively, he covered her hand with his. Before he could stop himself, he pulled her into his arms and pressed a soft, quick kiss to her mouth.

"I want to see more of you," he murmured, conscious of her nearness and the warmth of her breath against his skin as her chest heaved. "Promise me you'll think about going out with me."

She hesitated, pupils dilated, eyes fixed on his.

"Okay," she whispered, then opened the door and bolted, leaving him standing still, a tingly sensation on his lips, and a searing heat at the pit of his stomach.

CHAPTER SEVEN

Emem couldn't concentrate. As she sat inside the sound-proof radio booth listening to the soft music from Alicia Keys, her mind spun several miles per minute.

She'd just given a female caller advice about oral sex, extremely conscious of the fact that Yomi might have been listening to every word she'd said.

That thought had made her even more reckless, bolder than she'd ever been on the radio. Since her evening in his flat, she couldn't stop thinking about him. The sexy smile he'd repeatedly flashed that gave her a glimpse of stunning dimples on his perfectly chiselled cheeks. His audacious male arrogance. And most of all, the fact that the age difference between them hadn't made him flinch.

She'd never dated a younger man. Never even considered it. Her first boyfriend from university had been a year older. She'd thought him immature and had broken up with him for his childishness. From then on, she'd vowed never to date anyone who wasn't at least a few years older. With a four-year age gap ahead of her, Ejike had been a welcome change.

Until he cheated on you with a much younger woman. The unexpected thought made her stomach roil. It had been three weeks since she'd left him, and he'd not bothered coming after her. She wasn't sure yet if she felt relieved or hurt.

Well, to Hell with him. If he could have a younger woman, why couldn't she date a younger man? What was the harm in enjoying a young, virile man who wanted her? And she wanted him back, too. Had spent the past few days dreaming about him and her in more intimate positions than she believed possible.

All she could think about was the brief kiss they'd shared, his smell, that perfect blend of perspiration and cologne that made her want to swipe her tongue all over his smooth golden skin. Not so smooth, though—there were sparse, dark hairs on his forearms, and she had glimpsed a bit on his chest, too. She wanted to glide her palms down his skin and feel those hairs under her finger tips.

Blood flowed to her groin, heating up her core. She shifted in her seat. How could she feel this way about a twenty-something-year-old man? Why was she even so concerned about their age difference? Should it matter?

For once in her life, she could just throw caution to the wind, be her alter ego Sasha, and go with the flow. Enjoy a fling with a young male in his prime. They didn't have to be anything more than secret lovers, did they? The idea of a taboo sexual rendezvous with Yomi sent a shudder of excitement cascading down her spine.

"There's a call coming through, Sasha," Nnenna, her producer, announced, her shrill voice through the headphones piercing her thoughts.

Giving her a thumbs up, Emem lowered the volume of the music and pressed the flashing button on the switchboard.

"Hello, lover, welcome to *Late Nights with Sasha* on Mainland 106.2 FM. What's your name, and where are you calling from?"

"I'm Yomi from Apapa."

She stiffened as the raspy baritone that could only belong to one person resounded in her ears, transmitting a jolt of electricity all over her body.

Her breath caught in her throat, and she had to keep her mouth parted so she could continue to breathe.

Seconds ticked by as she tried to gain control of her wayward heart which drummed fast like a disco beat.

"Hello?" Yomi's hesitant voice came again, snapping her back into the moment.

"Hi, Yomi from Apapa," she said, regaining her composure, and ignoring the look of surprise on her producer's face pressed against the transparent glass wall separating them. "Thanks for calling *Late Nights with Sasha*—your safe haven to find answers to your relationship or sex problems. How can I help you tonight?"

"Well, Sasha, I'm very attracted to a woman who lives in my building. She is a beauty with a lovely personality, and has the sexiest smile ever."

A slow heat glided down her body at the huskiness of his voice. *Oh, Lord.* Emem rested her palm on her forehead in a feeble attempt to cool the fire burning her face.

"I want to get to know her better, and I sense that she is attracted to me, too. But when I asked her out, she declined."

From the corner of her eye, she detected that Nnenna had risen from her seat, all attention now focused on her, causing a nervous anxiety to grip her gut.

"Did she give you a reason?" Emem asked, trying to sound as professional as she could, despite the volcano of emotions erupting in her veins.

"Yes, she did. Two, actually. She says I'm too young for her, and that she's not interested in dating so soon after a recent break-up."

"Maybe she needs time to come around," she said.

"Or maybe ..." He paused, and she held her breath, both anticipating and dreading his next comment. "But maybe she is just scared ... scared of taking a chance on what could be an exciting journey for both of us."

Seconds of silence followed.

"So, my question is, Sasha, what can I do to convince her that our age difference doesn't mean anything to me? And that I'm serious about wanting to get to know her better, spend more time with her, and not just for the fun of it."

Emem sat upright. The determination in his tone and his words caused her heart to fibrillate at an alarmingly dangerous rate. A gentle tap on the transparent glass attracted her attention to her producer who regarded her with bewilderment.

"Answer him," Nnenna mouthed, her forehead creased up in mild irritation.

She nodded in response.

"Yomi, eh ... I think you should show her, instead of telling her. Find out why she is scared about opening up to you," Emem replied. "You should try gentle persuasive gestures. She may want to be with you, too, but may be wary due to previous relationship problems."

"Hmm ... great idea," he said. "What kind of gestures do you suggest?"

"She lives in your apartment building, doesn't she?"

"Yes, she does."

"Good. Maybe bring her dinner on your way from work. When in doubt, food always works."

His low chuckle filtered through the speakers, and a reflex smile touched her lips.

"Try friendly chats when you bump into her in the hallway. Build up a friendship first. And when you've gained her trust, probe—find out her fears about being in a relationship with a younger man and think about what you can do to dispel them."

"Great advice, Sasha. Thank you. I'm feeling more inspired. One way or another, I'm going to make sure this amazing woman takes a chance on us."

Silence.

Her stomach jumped, perspiration damp under both arms, and the air-conditioning in the room seemed grossly inadequate at the moment.

"You're welcome. Thanks for calling in, Yomi. Glad to be of help. Wishing you all the best in your quest to win her over."

"Thanks, Sasha. And see you soon."

The line went dead. For moments, she sat still, immobilised by both shock and excitement.

"See you soon."

His final words echoed in her head. Her body trembled all over. He would be persistent. Which usually irritated her. Why did the thought not make her as exasperated as she should be?

Another soft knock on the glass separating her producer's booth from hers made her jump. She gave Nnenna an apologetic look.

"Thanks for listening, lovers. Keep your dial on 106.2 as we go into commercial break. When we come back, we'll talk more about age difference and dating," she said, pressing down the controller knob.

As the bubbly commercial jingle floated through the room, she spun her chair towards Nnenna.

"Sorry, I was—"

"Ha! Sorry *ke*?" Nnenna shook her head. "*Biko*, give me the details about this Yomi fellow that called just now. You've been keeping secrets from me *abi*?"

"No, nothing like that." She giggled.

"It's not nothing. See how you are blushing like a goat," Nnenna snorted, walking over from her booth to join her.

"Goats don't blush ..."

"*Biko*, focus. Who is he? Is he asking you out? And are you saying no?" Nnenna's false eyelashes batted against her cheeks as she spoke. "Why say no to him after what your asshole boyfriend did to you? Talk now, or I'll be on your ass all night."

"Okay, okay. He's a guy who lives upstairs in my apartment building. He asked me out. I said no, end of story."

"Which *kain* end of story? Why didn't you agree to go out with him? Is he ugly? Or aren't you feeling him?"

"Oh, I'm feeling him, alright. He's gorgeous."

"So, what's the problem?"

"He is almost ten years younger than me, *mbok*."

"So?" The incredulous expression on Nnenna's face made her lips spread into a grin as she recalled that same expression on Yomi's face when she'd given that excuse.

"I don't know. I'm not a cradle snatcher."

"*Biko*, snatch his cradle. If a man is ten years older than his love interest, it wouldn't be considered cradle snatching, would it? And he certainly would not be called a cougar," Nnenna said, resting a hand on her hip. "Society makes life so difficult for women sometimes. Why can't you live your life and give this guy a chance? Heck, Ejike didn't think twice about dating a woman almost half his age while still in a relationship with you."

Emem remained silent, mulling Nnenna's words.

"You're right, ma," she agreed, finally finding in her boss's words the courage she needed to take a leap and break out of her self-imposed inhibitions.

CHAPTER EIGHT

Yomi couldn't help the pride that swelled his chest at the massive turn-out at the awards ceremony to celebrate the artistic talents of young Apapa residents. And he was a part of it all, seated at the chairperson's table.

His gaze swept over the ten finalists standing on the podium. As they held their prizes, a sense of fulfilment filled him. The winners had not only each been given a cheque for a hundred thousand Naira, but also a scholarship to the Nigerian federal university of their choice.

Since the vast majority of the contestants came from disadvantaged backgrounds, this was a great opportunity, the only real hope of higher education for most of them.

"To all of you who took part in this exercise—well done," complimented Peter Edwards.

Yomi liked the American immigrant who'd founded the Apapa Youth Project (AYP). Such faith in African youth, and Peter put his time and energy where his mouth was. It was inspiring how he encouraged and pushed young people to do their best.

"Even if you didn't win today, you are a winner. Keep working hard, keep getting involved in our activities. Your participation is greatly appreciated."

Loud applause followed, and Yomi found himself clapping vigorously, too.

He'd met Peter when he'd first moved to Apapa, full of vigour and a need to integrate with the local community. That meeting had changed his view about Nigeria and the gross inequality between rich and poor.

As he'd driven him around the slums of Apapa, Peter had suggested that one of the best ways to make a difference while mingling with people included participating in projects such as this. Without needing much convincing, Yomi had joined Peter's pioneering project to empower young people to get an education, and he'd never regretted it.

During four years of working with a team of other dedicated activists, they'd managed to rescue a few young people from the clutches of poverty, drugs, and gang-related crime in the community. He knew fourteen of them currently spread across federal universities because of this initiative.

"Thanks to everyone for making this happen. All the donors, the participants, and the team who scored the competitions." Peter turned to the chair table and bowed his head. "Thank you, Yomi, Chichi, Folarin, and Mohammed for your hard work as dedicated judges."

A deafening standing ovation ensued.

"Let's celebrate this Saturday with food, drink, dancing, and merriment made available by the one and only local government chairman, Mr. Momodu."

Following a loud drumroll bang, cheering and music from the deejay resounded in the room.

Still in high spirits, Yomi rose from his seat, embraced his fellow judges, and strolled down the platform, ready to mingle with the crowd.

Hours later and feeling refreshed, he took a walk back home from the venue only about twenty minutes away. He had not driven here because he'd wanted to exercise his muscles a bit, having missed his usual morning run so he could join other volunteers to organise the event.

As he pushed open the front entrance of his apartment building, a distinct flowery scent enveloped him, and his lips curved into a half-smile. Totally unbelievable how without even seeing Emem, he could tell her scent from miles away. She'd just passed through this hallway. Inhaling deeply, he walked past her front door, hesitated for seconds, and then strolled away.

"Don't be a stalker, Yomi," he muttered to himself, quashing the impulse to knock on her door. He needed to be more organised about wooing her. And he had begun formulating a plan.

The impromptu telephone call he'd made to the radio station last night had been insightful. He wouldn't ruin his plans of winning Emem over by knocking on her door unexpectedly despite the temptation to see her face.

No, he'd wait for the flowers he'd ordered from the local florist to arrive at her door, and then wait for her response. Hopefully, the glamourous display of lilies and daffodils would make her smile and bring her closer to accepting his advances.

After a quick shower, he settled on the sofa, hoping to catch up with his favourite TV series, *Game of Thrones*. Just as he lifted the remote from the wooden holder anchored to the corner of the couch, his doorbell chimed.

Startled, he jumped up. His eyes darted to the silver digital clock on the wall. Six-thirty p.m. He wasn't expecting anyone.

Ambling towards the door, a thought occurred to him, and he grinned. His brother had an annoying habit of visiting without invitation.

"Kunle, na you *dey* there?" he asked, preparing to tell him off.

"No, it's Emem."

He froze. The unexpectedness and joy of hearing her husky voice caused his heart to gallop.

"Emem?"

"Yes, can I come in?"

He unlocked the door eagerly. "Of course."

"Sorry I came uninvited, but I just saw you walk in."

"You are welcome here anytime," he said, stepping away from the door. "Please come in."

She hesitated. "Are you sure? I can come back if you're busy."

"I'm sure. Come on in."

Giving him a shy smile, she sauntered into his apartment. As she walked past, a whiff of her fragrance floated into his nostrils, spreading warmth over him.

After a few steps, she turned towards him.

"I ... eh ..." she began, running her fingers over her closely cropped curls.

His gaze followed her movement, and once again, he marvelled at her perfectly oval-shaped face. With softened cheekbones and well-carved full lips, she pulled off the almost-bald-chick look effortlessly. Completely devoid of makeup, and dressed in blue denim trouser dungarees, she looked so much younger than her age.

"Is ... is the date offer still open?"

Her tentative question brought his focus back to her eyes. She appeared flustered, fidgeting with the buckle over her chest.

His heart fluttered. "Yes. Yes, of course."

"Okay, then. I'll go out with you."

Relief flooded his senses, so profound that he couldn't stem the grin that spread across his face.

"That's great, Emem. That's awesome," he enthused. Then, pointing to the sofa he'd just vacated, he added, "Would you like to sit down, so we can talk about it?"

Her posture relaxed, and she smiled. "Yes, thanks."

"Would you like something to eat? Drink?"

She shook her head before settling on the sofa. "No, thanks. Just ate dinner."

"So early?" he asked, taking the seat across from her. "I usually have mine around ten."

"What? That's too late. If I do that, I'll put on weight, and I can't afford to, the rate at which I'm doubling in size."

His gaze trailed slowly down her body, appreciating the curves her baggy outfit couldn't quite contain. Full breasts, a fuller ass. Perfection. He loved the meat on her, soft and round in the right places.

"Your figure's perfect, Emem," he remarked, bringing his attention back to her face. "You should never even worry about losing any weight."

"Th ... thanks," she gulped, lowering her lashes. "I have already agreed to go out with you, Yomi, so you don't have to flatter me."

"Flatter you?" he interjected, his voice uncontrollably hoarse. "Never. That's the God-honest truth." He paused, gaze fixed on her, waiting until she raised her eyes to meet his. "Oh, Emem, I wish you could see yourself through my eyes. You're unbelievably sexy. I haven't been able to stop thinking about you since the first day I saw you."

Her back stiffened, and a small gasp escaped her lips. She opened her mouth as though preparing to respond. However, she said nothing.

He could tell his brazen comment had stunned her. A reflex need to apologise for his blatant leering and the way his words had somewhat objectified her body rose within him, but he stifled that instinct. He wanted no ambiguity about his interest in her, no room to be friend-zoned by her because of any inhibitions she may have about dating him. And he intended to make it clear he desired her as a woman, not as a buddy to hang out with.

"Yes, Emem. I'm not playing games here. This date? We are going out as a man and a woman. Not as neighbours. Not as friends. It's a real date. Okay?"

She remained silent.

"Okay?" he asked again.

"Okay."

He released a relieved breath. "Good. Because I'm serious about wanting to know you better. Are you down with that?"

She averted her gaze from his, focused her attention on her palms as they smoothed down the fabric of her attire, and then slowly raised her eyes to meet his squarely, all hesitation gone.

"Yes," she whispered, her tone raspy. "But I want to take things slowly. I don't want to move too fast."

"I'll take things as slowly as you want. There's all the time in the world for us."

"Okay, then. What do you have in mind for our first date?"

He hesitated, savouring her use of the word 'our.' It showed she was beginning to accept the idea of them dating.

"Let's see ... should we do the traditional movie then dinner? Or should we try something a bit more unconventional?"

"Like what?"

"There's a musical pantomime running three evenings a week for the next three months at a theatre. It's based off the novel *The Concubine* by Elechi Amadi. I hear it's amazing. My brother has seen it. I was planning to pop in one of these evenings. It would be nice to go together."

"That sounds like fun. I enjoyed the book when I read it years ago."

"Me, too. And the play adaptation has received amazing reviews. Linda Okoye is playing Ihuoma, and she's really good."

"Yes, she is. Her acting is so refreshingly natural." Emem's eyes sparkled as she spoke. "I'm in."

"Fantastic. We could have dinner after. I know a restaurant near the theatre offering a wide range of tasty meals."

She nodded. "That's fine."

"Cool, let me look at the available dates, so we could book in advance."

Yomi rose from his seat and strolled over to the wooden cabinet beside the television. He pulled out a sleek laptop and walked back towards her.

"May I sit next to you?" he asked, indicating with his finger the free space beside the sofa where she sat.

Nodding again, she slid across the leather seat, giving him more room.

Inhaling deeply, he settled beside her, supressing the urge to press his face against her skin and sniff the tantalising aroma that she exuded. She smelt heavenly. Like summer and rain.

Grinning at his poetic foolishness, he pulled open the laptop and pushed down the power button. As they waited in silence for it to turn on, he angled his head sideways and flashed her a smile.

"What's your last name?" he asked without preamble, although he had been curious about it since he'd met her. "You're from Akwa Ibom. So, I've been on Google searching for Efik last names, trying to guess yours."

Her laughter rang out, infectious, drawing him in. He couldn't help but join in, enjoying the view of her even white teeth.

"Hmm ... so what top three names did you come up with from your research?"

He hesitated, trailing a finger over his jaw thoughtfully.

"Let's see ... Bassey, Akpan, and Okon are the most popular."

"Oh, my God!" She covered her face with her palms, body quaking in giggles.

"What? Did I get it right?"

She nodded vigorously. "I swear down! I'm Emem Akpan. Oh, Lord, Google is the best. I have many cousins who are Okons and Basseys. This is hilarious."

"Truly," he agreed with a laugh. Seconds of silence followed. "Emem Akpan," he said, rolling the name off his tongue. "I love your name."

"Thanks, Yomi ...?"

"Oladipo," he supplied.

"From the popular Oladipo family?" she asked, her eyebrow arched in question.

He chuckled. "Popular? I don't know about that."

"Come on. Your father is always in the news and rubbing shoulders with prominent politicians and the crème de la crème of society. And your brother, Kunle ... isn't he dating that famous Brazilian model? What's her name?"

"Stacey Lopez. But they've broken up. He is now with the Ghanaian actress, Nana Foyle," Yomi answered, rolling his eyes. His brother had a thing for celebrities.

She let out a short laugh that ended in a rather unladylike snort. He loved that about her. Her reactions were genuine, completely unguarded.

"I love reading gossip blogs. Linda Ikeji's my favourite. And your brother's love life is very entertaining."

Yomi smiled. He agreed.

"You seem so different from your family. I've never even seen pictures of you in those celebrity scenes."

He shrugged noncommittally. "I'm not into all that stuff. I prefer a quiet and simple life."

"I can tell. You live here, and they live way up in Banana Island."

"To be honest, I hate those lavish parties organised solely to waste money and show wealth. I always make excuses not to attend. My father keeps telling me off about it, saying we need to keep active socially so we can procure more clients. I just don't get it, though. It's simply not my scene."

He wasn't like his family who enjoyed being the centre of news articles and parties. He preferred a modest lifestyle. And he liked working for his money. Although he had a substantial share of inheritance in the eventuality of his father passing away, he didn't want to rely on that. He wanted to make a name for himself, and so he saved money, not spending lavishly living a false life while awaiting his inheritance.

"I understand. I'm also nothing like my family."

"And what's your family like?"

She stiffened. Her gaze suddenly moved to the screen.

"The computer's on now, so we can book the seats," she said, the abrupt change in subject a clear sign that she didn't want to talk about her background.

That made him even more curious. What didn't she want him to know?

Deciding he could curtail his curiosity and wait until she trusted him enough, he redirected his attention on the computer screen between them.

"What do you think about next Saturday evening?" he asked her, scrolling the website's booking calendar.

"That's fine by me. Let's reserve the middle seat. It's still available." She made a move to get up. "I'll go get my card ..."

"No, I'll pay," he objected, clutching her arm to stop her.

The satiny skin beneath his palm enticed him, tempting him to glide his hand along its soft smoothness. A jolt of awareness passed through him. His groin twitched.

"I don't mind paying my half ..." Her voice fractured his sensual thoughts.

"I do. First date. I pay. Simple," he said, still holding onto her, knowing he should let go but unwilling to.

"I really don't mind ... I'm not one of those women who don't pay for stuff."

"I believe that. But I'll pay this time. You can pay for our next date."

She smiled as she settled back in the seat, this time closer to him than she'd been earlier. "Next date, huh? You're pretty confident about that."

Her body was inclined so that her shoulder touched his. Her left knee also grazed his. She appeared relaxed, cosy even, like she belonged in his apartment, in his life. Joy flooded his senses. He was a step closer to winning her over.

"Oh, yes, I am. I never stop until I get what I want."

"And what do you want?"

Her voice held a sultry timbre that hooked him, making him ache to pull her into his arms and kiss her senseless. However, he resisted the temptation. It would be too soon and may scare her off.

"You as my woman," he answered hoarsely, settling for the soothing feeling of her closeness instead.

Strange, he'd never believed in love at first sight. Yet, here he was already falling in love with Emem, and he knew it had started from the first time he'd heard her voice on the radio.

And me as your man, he added silently.

CHAPTER NINE

Sliding off her bra through her yellow cotton blouse, Emem sighed long and hard. What a busy day at the radio station. Although her show only aired Friday nights, part of her role as a General Manager involved producing other shows for Mainland FM.

Today, Cecilia Badmus, the main host for one of the station's most popular Monday morning show, *Breakfast with Cecilia*, had unexpectedly handed in her notice because she'd decided to relocate to Europe with her family. A major setback—she had been the anchor for nearly a decade.

In a state of panic, Emem had chaired several meetings, the job to find a replacement having been foisted on her. And the stress had been all the more heightened by the uncomfortable bra almost crushing her chest.

As she strolled to the wardrobe with the lacy brassiere hanging over her forearm, she massaged her breasts with her free palm. Having big breasts was all fun and games until one had to spend a whole day encased in a tight bra just to keep them upright and not jiggling all over the place.

Not for the first time, she longed for the small perky breasts that every other female in her family possessed. She shook her head as she recalled the period when she'd realised how much her physical appearance contrasted with her family's. Only fifteen years at the time, she had needed a D-Cup-sized bra; yet, her sister and mother, all petite with compact physiques, could walk about without one.

Growing up, she'd actually wondered if she were adopted because she'd not only looked different from her family, but also felt like the odd one out.

The first of three siblings—one sister and one brother—born to the founders of a large Pentecostal church in Port Harcourt, she'd always been the rebel, questioning everything about religion. She'd never settled into the routine of prayers and fasting that her parents forced on the family and had often been caught doing the opposite of what she was told God expected of her.

Although she'd tried to fit in, she never had. Her inquisitive nature had made her challenge the words of the Bible, landing her severe punishment from her parents and school teachers on many occasions.

Eventually, she'd come to accept her difference from the family was not just because of her physical attributes, but her personality, too. She could never be like her slim, prim and proper sister married to a good Christian man with well-behaved children, or her brother who was now also a pastor in the family-owned ministry.

They were everything their parents hoped for, while she was the opposite—a disgrace who had renounced her faith and moved into *sinful* Lagos with a man.

Although she missed her family, she hated going back home and seeing the condemnation in their eyes, the disappointment. Especially from her father, who barely spoke to her except to tell her how much she'd wronged God. Whenever she'd asked him about the Bible, his answer had always been the same. "Believe every single word from the good book, and follow it. Or you will burn in Hell."

Except one time.

"Daddy, how can Mary have been a virgin and had a child? It's not possible, is it?"

The memory of asking that question was still tattooed in her brain. As was his response. No explanation, no legitimate answer to her question about his faith. Faster than the blink of an eye, she had found herself locked inside a bathroom for hours. All for daring to ask why he believed that Jesus could be born from a virgin—the memory still stung. Her punishment had only ended when she had finally acquiesced to believing the gospel about the miraculous birth.

Henceforth, she'd stopped asking questions, drifting further and further away from her family. Her decision to relocate to Lagos to live with Ejike had been easy to make. Nothing but disenchantment remained at home for her, and visiting for family events had become more of a chore that she performed dutifully, staying a few days in a hotel before escaping as soon as she could.

The loud banging on her door interrupted her reflective thoughts. She paused halfway in pulling her shirt over her head.

Suppressing a sigh, Emem pulled her shirt back down over her head and strolled to the door. She wasn't expecting anyone, but hoped it was Yomi. She hadn't seen him for three days, and every time she left her apartment, she had to keep herself from climbing up the stairs to knock on his door.

That would only make her look like a stalker. She'd already visited his apartment uninvited twice. No way could she explain away a third visit. Although she missed his company, the next time she found herself in there, it had to be by invitation. So, she'd just have to wait for him to reach out to her.

They'd exchanged a few text messages about planning for their date, but nothing else, and it was eating her inside. Though she'd asked him to take

69

things slowly with her, there was a part of her that hoped he wouldn't.

"Who is it?" she called out, holding onto the door handle hesitantly.

"You have a delivery, ma," a croaky voice answered.

Definitely not Yomi's velvety baritone.

"What kind of delivery? I didn't order anything."

"Flowers, ma." The voice came again, sounding impatient.

"Okay."

Emem turned the security lock anti-clockwise and opened the door slightly. Still unsure, she peeked through the small gap between them, and her jaw popped open.

A stunning bouquet greeted her eyes. She rested her attention on the beautiful yellow and white flower petals wrapped in a purple silk bow, barely acknowledging the middle-aged delivery man holding it out to her.

"This is for you, ma," the slender man said, hand still outstretched. He shoved a small electronic gadget in his other hand to her. "Can you sign here?"

She quickly snapped out of her shock.

"Y-Yes, thank you," she sputtered, scribbling down her signature with a finger, and then accepting the flowers from him.

"Good day, madam," he said before strolling away.

With excitement spiralling down her body, Emem pulled out a small card tucked neatly inside the delicately wrapped floral arrangement.

Can't wait for our first date, I hope it's as wonderful as I've dreamed it to be.
Thinking about you constantly.
Yomi

An uncontrollable smile split her face as she stood by the door, holding the card against her thumping heart for moments. She sniffed the flowers and inhaled deeply. *Fabulous.*

The lovely fragrance took her breath away. She'd never received flowers from anyone in her life. Not even Ejike.

Still beaming from ear to ear, she moved over to the kitchen and pulled open a cabinet below the sink. She scanned the contents of the space, searching for a suitable storage container.

"Perfect," she murmured, lifting a shallow ceramic bowl from the far end of the cluttered cupboard. With no flower vase anywhere in the house, this would have to do.

Whistling, she filled the bowl halfway with tap water, unwrapped the bouquet, and then arranged the flowers in the bowl. Satisfied, she leaned back and admired the arrangement of lilies and daffodils.

The brilliant display brought another flush to her face, unabashedly thrilled to be the object of interest of a young sexy male. It felt good to be wooed by a man, an experience she'd never had.

Her university boyfriend had been a study partner who she'd eventually started dating. And when that hadn't worked out, she had jumped on a chance at a relationship with Ejike to escape from her family and everything she'd felt had been holding her back.

Ejike had not pursued her much. In fact, she'd been so afraid of being alone and stuck at home that, without much of an effort from him, she had uprooted her life to follow him to the other end of the country.

Thinking about it now, she realised her previous relationships had felt like a journey and not a destination, as though she had been searching for something more. What—she couldn't quite say. But something ...

However, Yomi made her feel free, enthusiastic, like a teenager being romanced by her crush. And it was a heady sensation.

She rushed to her room, unzipped her bag, and retrieved her mobile phone. Without thinking about it, she dialled Yomi's number. It rang twice before the line connected.

"Hello, beautiful."

His deep voice floated in her ear, spreading goose bumps over her skin.

"Hi, Yomi, thanks for the amazing flowers. They are so beautiful."

"You are welcome, Emem."

She imagined him smiling and could almost picture his dimples deepening as his full lips parted. Her abdominal muscles contracted. What she wouldn't give to flick her tongue over those stunning crevices on his face.

"So, it's just two days left 'til our date. I can't wait," he said, breaking through her sensual thoughts.

Her cheeks heated up. "I can't wait, either. I've bought three dresses. Not sure which to choose."

His low chuckle filtered through the phone earpiece.

"Although I would love to see you in a dress, you don't need to stress out about what to wear. You look good in anything."

His compliment made her giddy with happiness. Resting a palm on her belly, she attempted to quell the nervous excitement rippling through her by blowing out a slow breath.

"Thank you, Yomi. Still, I want to look hot."

"Ouch! I hope I can handle the heat."

"I hope so, too ... 'cos this Saturday, I'm coming out dressed to kill and blazing with fire."

His deep groan echoed in her ear, sending her pulse rate sky-high.

"Why are you doing this to me?"

"Doing what?" she asked sweetly, although she could hear the heavy pounding of her own heart.

This was so unlike her. Totally different from her usual guardedness. Here she was, flirting with a man over the phone, being the bold and daring Sasha she'd only let loose on the radio show. A facet of her personality that she never showed others because of her religious background.

"You know what you're doing, girl. Testing me, trying to make me break my resolve not to come pounding on your door before our date. And I'm trying hard to be a gentleman and stick to the plan."

"The plan ... what plan?"

"The slow and steady plan."

She giggled. "You can stick to that slow and steady path. But know that I also have plans of my own, Mister."

"Yeah? I'd love to hear all about them. But when we are on our date, that is."

A smile lifted the corner of her lips. "Hmm, a patient man ... the kind of man I love."

He didn't respond. Seconds of silence ensued. Emem reclined against the wall as she fiddled with the front zipper of her black skirt.

Suddenly worried she had ruined the moment by mentioning the word 'love,' she leaned forward.

"Yomi?"

"Emem." His voice sounded hoarse. "I'll be patient until you can say that to me and mean it."

Her breath hitched. She was rendered speechless by his words and raspy tone. Moments ticked by. This

73

was certainly no longer easy flirting, and she didn't know how to respond to that comment. Having never been in this situation, she searched her brain for something carefree to say, a phrase her alter ego would use to lighten the mood, but nothing came to mind.

"Emem, how was your day?"

His relaxed tone and the sudden change of subject took her worries away. He sounded breezy and back to his usual cheerful self.

"Hectic," she answered, happy to steer clear of deep emotions. "A major anchor has put in her resignation, and I am responsible for either replacing her or creating a replacement show. I'm not sure yet what to settle on."

"It's always difficult making changes. How did you go about tackling the issue?"

Sliding her back down the wall to sit on the floor, she proceeded to fill him in on the stressful day she'd had.

***

Gaze glued to the full-length mirror by her dressing table, Emem swiped red lipstick across her lips. Twisting the small tube closed and replacing the cap, she straightened her back and studied the final product of nearly an hour of fussing over her appearance.

"Not bad for a rush job," she murmured, running her palms down the sides of her dress as she eyed her reflection in the mirror.

Yesterday, she'd been at the studio overnight for her show and had immediately fallen asleep when she'd gotten home.

There hadn't been much time to dwell on preparation for her date with Yomi until two hours ago, when she'd awoken from deep slumber.

Scrambling from bed in a state of panic, she had dashed into the bathroom for a quick shower. Still indecisive about what to wear, she'd changed three times before settling on what she had on now.

A light tapping on the door caused her heart to jump. Her gaze dashed to the clock over the rumpled, moderate-sized bed she'd recently awoken from. Four-thirty p.m. Yomi was here and right on time.

She checked her reflection in the mirror once more and sighed. Although she liked the fit of the red, ankle-length gown, she worried that her voluptuous body made it look a tad tacky, like she was vying for attention. The side slit that reached mid-thigh didn't help, either.

Maybe I should change.

Another soft tap on the door crushed that idea.

"I'll be right there," she answered, making a final adjustment to the round loop earring on her left ear. This was it. Her first date with Yomi. And for some odd reason, she had set such a high standard for today that it now made her anxious.

Sucking in a calming breath, she turned away from the mirror and sauntered towards the front door.

"Yomi?" she called at the door, stalling to steady her nerves, although she knew it was him.

"Yes, beautiful."

His eager response from behind the door increased her anxiety.

What if he took one look at her and lost interest? What if after all her bragging about looking hot and fiery for the date, she ended up appearing uninspiring to him? Why did she even care so much?

Her doubts immediately vanished when she opened the door. The intense fire in his eyes as his gaze trailed over her attire slowly made her blood heat up and sent her pulse rate into overdrive.

"Oh, Emem ..." He placed a palm over his chest. "You look exquisite. This dress ... excellent choice.

Your hair, and your face ... everything. You're beautiful ... perfect."

His deep voice and the earnest way the compliments spewed out of his mouth sent a flash of excitement simmering all over her. Yomi had a way of boosting her ego, making her feel sexy with his eyes and words. So intoxicating.

"Thanks, Yomi. And you look amazing, too," she replied, face flushing from both pleasure and anticipation. Now, she couldn't wait to share the evening, and perhaps, if all went well, the night with him.

"I love your shirt. The red and white pattern suits your skin tone."

Although she knew she was babbling, she couldn't help herself. He looked yummy. Always did. The way his muscles bulged from the short-sleeved, tropical-print shirt exuded youthful masculinity. The graphic tattoos visible on both arms lent him an edgy look. And with his dreadlocks hanging freely down his shoulders, he looked virile, and she itched to run her fingers through the long locks while she sat astride his jean-clad, muscular thighs.

"Thanks. But all I can say is, I'm glad to be the one by your side this evening."

His smooth baritone interrupted her carnal thoughts, making her blush even harder.

"These are for you," he added, a lop-sided grin on his lips.

Her gaze dropped to the bouquet of roses in his hand, which she hadn't even noticed earlier while busy ogling him.

"Oh, thanks, they are lovely," she gushed, taking the beautiful red flowers from him. "Smell amazing, too."

Just like you.

"Come on in." She stepped aside to give him room. "I'll put this in a vase and grab my purse."

Yomi strode into her apartment confidently, sweeping his gaze around.

"Nice place. It's amazing how different decorating styles make two exactly alike rooms look completely unlike each other."

"True. Your apartment seems so different from mine, although they are built exactly the same. I repainted the walls dark blue. I prefer subdued colours to bright walls or décor."

He chuckled, moving farther into the room and standing under the only painting on her wall. "It's obvious. Even this painting is of a dark forest. There's something gloomy about it … yet, it's captivating. I love it. Do you know the artist?"

Emem shook her head. "Nope. To be honest, I bought it from a roadside hawker for about three thousand Naira. I haven't even given it much thought. I just wanted a painting in my sitting room."

He threw back his head and bellowed with laughter.

"Really?"

"Really," she chortled. "I'm the least art-inclined person out there."

"Oh, then we'll have to change that. I'm an art lover and collector. Looking forward to converting you."

"Don't hold your breath. I'm more into music."

"Is that why you have that?" He pointed to the large wooden grand piano taking up almost a quarter of the room. "Do you play?"

"Yes. But I haven't in a long while."

She lowered her lashes, unwilling to talk about the times when she used to immerse herself in the melodious sounds she produced from the keyboard. A time when her grandmother, the only person who really understood her, had been alive. Ma Josephine had been the one who'd taught her how to play the piano, and since her death seven years ago, she'd not been able to do so without crying. Therefore, she'd simply stopped.

"You okay?"

His concerned question brought her mind back.

Emem averted her eyes from the intense gaze boring into her.

"Yes, thanks," she replied with a smile.

Wanting to change the topic, she peeked at the bracelet watch on her wrist. "We should get going soon. Let me get my stuff so we can leave. Would you like anything to eat or drink before we head out?"

"No, thanks."

"Cool. Be back in a flash."

As she walked away with the bouquet in her hands, she felt his eyes piercing her back and instinctively knew his gaze was focused on her bottom.

Her dress, although not too tight, moulded over her behind. Inevitable because of the generous size of her ass. Self-conscious, yet somewhat thrilled, she swayed her hips a bit more eagerly with each step she took.

Just as she got to the door of the kitchen, she hazarded a quick glance at him and found his eyes fixed exactly where she'd expected them to be. Tickled by his blatant enthralment, she cleared her throat and slanted her lips into a knowing smile.

Yomi's gaze sprang back to her eyes, but he didn't appear embarrassed to be caught staring at her ass. Instead, he flashed her a wolfish grin.

"Take your time, beautiful. We have about an hour before the play starts," he murmured, completely unfazed as he sank onto a couch in the sitting room.

With a smile still plastered on her face, Emem strolled into the kitchen. She grabbed a plastic bowl from the lower cabinet, poured some water from the tap into it, and inserted the roses inside.

"You haven't unpacked fully," he commented as she returned from the kitchen.

"Nope." She followed his line of vision to the few clutters of labelled boxes, still unopened, at the corner of the room. "I've not yet made out time to organise things. And I hate unpacking."

"I could help, you know," he offered. "I enjoy decorating."

"Thanks, I'll keep that in mind."

She lowered the flowers on the centre of the oval dining table adjacent to the sitting room and lifted her purse from the seat beside it.

"I'm ready," she announced.

Yomi rose. His dark eyes travelled over her slowly, and he let out a low groan when they eased back to her face. "I wish I could say the same, girl. You are killing me in that dress."

Without responding, Emem sashayed ahead of him. She flipped her head over her shoulder when she got to the front door and offered him a sly smile.

"I aim to please," she whispered, hoping her voice sounded as sultry as she thought it did.

"Girl, don't be playing with fire."

"I am the fire, so I should be telling *you* that."

His deep laughter rumbled through her apartment, warming her insides. She enjoyed flirting with this man. It made her feel unrestricted, like a caged bird suddenly let free. She couldn't control the excitement this new adventure brought her.

For once in her adult life, she wasn't concerned about marriage, a future, but was in the here and now, enjoying the moment, just like she'd advised so many callers on the radio show.

"Okay, Miss Hottie, let's head out before this room combusts," he quipped, placing a palm at the small of her back as he accompanied her out of the apartment.

Emem settled into the front seat of his SUV feeling on top of the world and like a character in a romantic movie. A light affair with a younger man was all she needed to get her mojo back. And she resolved to enjoy all the attention from Yomi for as long as it lasted.

CHAPTER TEN

Seated beside Emem in the darkened theatre, Yomi leaned back, relishing the cool air from the air-conditioner vents in the ceiling that blew across his skin. The room was crammed with people. And though the plastic seats were small and slightly uncomfortable, they were adequately spaced apart, giving each individual a bit of room. Luckily, their centre seats gave them a great vantage point. A perfect view of the stage.

He cast a sidelong glance at Emem. Her rapt attention on the stage showed she was enjoying herself. Earlier on, he'd spied a tear drop spill from the corner of her eye when the main character Ihuoma's husband died.

He understood completely. The actress portraying Ihuoma inhabited the role so completely and with such vivid emotion, his own throat had choked up. He'd reached out and squeezed Emem's hand, impressed that she had not attempted to hide her response to that sorrowful scene.

A collective roar of laughter from the audience brought his attention to the actors on the podium. He immediately spotted the cause of the amusement. Emenike, the male main character who had become delirious from the effects of poison administered by his wife, was perched on a tree, refusing to climb down until his family fetched Ihuoma, his love interest.

Yomi chuckled at the hysterical way the actor clung to the synthetic tree branch, shaking his head vehemently and ignoring the entreaties of his family.

"This is one of my favourite parts of the book," Emem whispered into his ear. "I remember laughing out loud when I read this scene."

Her warm breath against his skin ignited a fiery path down his body, causing a flow of blood to tighten his groin. He shifted in his seat, glad for the semi-darkness that hid his uncontrollable physical response to her.

An intense desire to kiss her overwhelmed him, but he pushed back that need. His throat clogged with a fierce longing. He wished they were already past the tentative stage of their budding relationship, that he'd already succeeded in breaking down all the barriers in her head about being with him. If that were the case, pulling her in for a kiss would be the most natural thing for him to do at this very instant. Just like he ached to do now. He had to swallow hard before he could respond.

"I remember this part, too. Hilarious. And this actor is excellent. I haven't seen any of his previous work, so I wasn't sure what to expect. But he's given a stellar performance so far."

"Yes, he's been brilliant."

She blew out a happy sigh and inclined closer to him, her soft breasts pressed against his arm, so close, he could swear he felt her heartbeat reverberating against him.

"I'm having such an amazing time. Thanks for bringing me here," she murmured, brushing her lips against his cheek.

He froze, startled by the unexpected kiss. The muscles all over his body tensed as his gaze held hers. Even in the dim lighting, he could sense the atmosphere had changed between them.

He cleared his throat, which felt like a lump had lodged in there.

"You're welcome," he croaked, his voice raspy from the strain of fighting back his desire to kiss her. He wondered if it would be too soon if he did. They were in public. Would she find that sleazy?

Without any warning, she lifted her lips to his and kissed him on the mouth, ending all his concerns. Angling her head closer, she repeated the kiss. This time, her tongue flickered over his lower lip.

Suppressing a guttural groan, Yomi reached for her face and cupped it in both palms, lowering his mouth to hers. He swept his tongue into her opened mouth, testing, stroking its warm sweetness as he meshed their lips together. She tasted so good, like soda and candy.

Her tongue eagerly entwined with his, heating his blood, making him want to forget they were in public at the centre of a room full of people and drag her onto his lap.

A part of his brain warned him to slow down, that they may have an audience, but another primal part of him couldn't care less. He'd dreamed of this moment for weeks, longed to taste her succulent, full lips, and he'd be damned if anything stopped him now.

He heard her soft whimper as she clutched his locks in her fingers, drawing him closer for a deeper kiss. All rational thoughts scrambled from his brain. Groaning deeply, he swiped his tongue again over her bottom lip and then, the inner corner of both cheeks, savouring the flavours of passion from her wet mouth. He wanted to devour her, crawl into her skin …

A startling loud rumble of laughter resonated around them, crashing through his sensual fog. Breaking off the kiss, he held onto her face. He blew out shallow breaths from his parted lips as his tunnel vision narrowed on her, blocking out everyone else in the room. She appeared dazed, and somewhat embarrassed.

Not wanting her to regret her spontaneity, he raised his finger and brushed the side of her jaw tenderly.

"Thank you for that amazing kiss, Emem," he whispered hoarsely.

Her lips curved into a half smile that caused his chest to swell with relief. She didn't regret it. Her next words confirmed his deduction, and he relaxed.

"Pretty good, wasn't it?" Her eyes sparkled with the same teasing lightness as her words. "Thank you, too."

Draping an arm around her shoulders, he pulled her closer to him as they both redirected their attention on the stage.

Oblivious to the other occupants of the room, Yomi settled back onto his seat, content to be next to the only woman who made him feel genuinely happy.

*

CHAPTER ELEVEN

"I can't believe you remember that," Emem groaned, her face on fire. She still found it embarrassing that Yomi knew she was Sasha from Mainland FM.

They were seated across from each other at a secluded corner of *Wande* restaurant, a popular eatery in the town centre, sharing a bottle of Merlot while awaiting their meals. The play had ended twenty minutes ago, and they'd strolled over from the theatre straight away.

"I'll never forget your advice to that lady about talking dirty during sex. Oh, my goodness, I think my ears got pregnant from your words."

She flung her head back, roaring with laughter. Placing a palm over her mouth to stifle the noise, she directed a remorseful look at the two diners close by whose irate gazes had swung to her.

"Sorry," she muttered in apology, still shaking with laughter as they turned back to their dinner.

Yomi let out a hearty laugh, too.

"True, true … good advice, though. I'm sure the woman went home and made her partner a happy man."

"Honestly, this is still strange—meeting someone who knows I'm the one saying all that shit," she said when she finally got a hold of herself. "I run my mouth so much on that show *sha*."

Yomi raised his glass of wine to his lips and took a quick sip, his eyes brimming with amusement. "I wouldn't call it running your mouth. You're brilliant, Emem, and I like the way you don't shy away from talking about sex the way many people in this country do."

Her cheeks warmed up at his compliment. Apart from her friend Natalie, nobody had ever praised her directly about her show. Yes, there'd been the occasional email or letter of commendation, but it felt good to hear it face to face.

"I've listened to *Late Nights with Sasha* religiously, and every time, I'm impressed by your insight."

His deep voice broke through her musings.

"Thank you so much. It means a lot to me." She paused and sipped from her wine glass. "So, I've been curious to know. How did you stumble upon my show? I mean, most of my callers are females, so I'm always surprised whenever a man calls."

Yomi hesitated, eyes focused downward on his finger tracing multiple circles over the table. For a brief moment, Emem thought he hadn't heard her, and she was about to repeat her question. But then, he raised his gaze to hers once again.

"That was the evening when I had to wait for hours at the police station to report the conman that scammed me. As I sat at a corner of the untidy cubicle, I had to put on my earphones so I could block the noise around me. It was a new phone with none of my music collection downloaded, so I turned on the radio. And voila, there was your lovely voice."

Her heart began to thump faster as he spoke. She couldn't believe it. On his first day back to Nigeria, he'd caught her show. That was also her first week as an anchor. She'd been employed on a one-month trial basis and had been persistently nervous until she had signed the two-year contract guaranteeing her job.

"You were giving advice to a widow worried about her first sexual relationship seven years after her husband's death. I won't forget what you said to her."

His tone was deep and reflective, and she found herself hanging onto every word he said, holding her breath as though he would discontinue his recount if she so much as breathed. "You said, 'your body won't suddenly shut down because your mind has. Give it what it needs, and your mind will follow'."

"Wow," she murmured, her throat suddenly tight. The look of awe reflected in Yomi's eyes was priceless, rewarding. She swallowed hard. "I can't even remember saying that."

"Oh, but I'll never forget the effect of those words on me. After hearing that comment, I straightened my back and vowed to stop feeling sorry for myself about the embarrassment of being duped. Since that Friday night, I haven't missed a show. You're amazing."

"T-thanks," she choked out, a slow warmth seeping down her bones at his moving commendation. "I've never heard someone say anything so touching about my work, never really thought about my advice on the show helping anyone, much less inspiring someone."

And that was true. She loved her job, but to be honest, the many negative feedback by irate members of the public writing to the station with complaints about her show being a pollution to the minds of youths and calling her a filthy, sex-obsessed whore, amongst other unsavoury names, discouraged her tremendously.

She'd become a bit flippant and sometimes gave her advice to callers without much thought. To realise that there were people who could actually make life-altering changes because of her show was humbling.

"You're welcome, Emem, but I'm only saying the truth."

"It's nice to hear positive feedback. Believe me, the judgemental letters I get about the show are overwhelming."

"I know. I've heard a few callers who you've had to cut off because of their rudeness."

"And they are so hypocritical. Despite the disapproval from the public, the ratings keep rising, and my audience grows by impressive numbers every week. That's why I'm still on air. And keep getting renewed yearly."

"Good for you, beautiful." He raised his glass to hers in salute.

Giving him a grateful smile, she clinked her glass with his. "Thanks."

Yomi returned her smile and took a sip of his drink. "So, how did you get involved in relationship advice? What started all this?"

Emem paused. It was a long story. There was the semi-honest version she'd provided in her book—her desire to help people with sexual problems because she'd faced similar issues—and the true reason.

Gazing into his intense eyes, she knew she had to be honest with him. He had a way of making her feel he could read her soul, and she sensed lying to him would be tricky.

"Do you know anything about True Faith Ministries?"

Yomi shook his head, forehead crinkled in confusion. "No. Is that a church?"

"Yes. Actually, a large church with the headquarters located in Port Harcourt and with several branches all over Nigeria. The founder, Bishop Akpan, is my father."

The name and title seemed to spark a recognition in his eyes. He opened his mouth as though ready to respond, but shut it when a waitress approached their table carrying two steaming plates in both hands. They simultaneously turned their attention to her.

"Your food is ready, Sir, and Ma," she said, her lips spread in a practiced grin.

"Thanks ... smells good," Yomi said, flashing her a dimpled smile.

The young lady, who looked captivated by him, blushed as she set his plate of fried rice and roasted turkey in front of him.

"Thank you, Sir. Hope you enjoy it." Turning to Emem, the waitress lowered her plate of gizzard *jollof* rice a lot less enthusiastically. "Enjoy your food, Ma."

Emem suppressed the need to roll her eyes.

"I will," she replied, hoping her tone didn't reveal the irritation rising within her.

The waitress turned back to Yomi, giving him a wink. "Please let me know if you need anything else, Sir. My name is Lovett, and I'm at your service." Her words came out in a slurred, sultry lilt, 'anything' sounding like 'arytin.'

Yomi reached out to clasp Emem's hand. "We will."

Emem found herself smiling at the defeated look that settled on the young waitress' pretty face as she strolled away.

For some reason she didn't want to analyse, that encounter made her insides burn with jealousy. Odd, considering she and Yomi were just on a first date and not really yet an item. But she despised the idea of another woman flirting with him. Especially right in front of her.

"This looks great," Yomi said, his attention already on his meal, as though he hadn't even noticed the not-so-subtle flirting by the waitress. "Can't wait to dig in."

"Me, too." She took a forkful of rice and moaned when the zesty flavours hit her palate. "Delicious and expertly seasoned," she gushed, nodding in approval.

Yomi lifted his fork to his mouth. She watched him chew slowly, his pupils gradually narrowing into appreciative slits as he swallowed.

"Perfect," he said. And scooped another bite from his plate. "This place has never let me down. The food is simply amazing."

"I agree. Now, I'll be driving here on my way from work to grab dinner anytime I'm feeling too lazy to cook."

He chuckled. "Or you could drop by my apartment. I am the best *ewedu* soup and okra soup cook ever."

"Really? You? Cook?"

"Oh, yes. And I make excellent roast dinners, too."

"Excellent? Such confidence. Now, I'm curious. I'll be sure to take you up on that offer."

"Please do. I bet after tasting my food, you'll want to move in with me," he chortled, and she grinned in response, pondering why at the moment, the idea of living with Yomi didn't sound as odd as she'd imagined it would.

Companionable silence settled between them while they concentrated on their meals, the sultry rhythm and blues music from the speakers in the brightly lit restaurant providing a soothing ambience.

"So, you were telling me about your reasons for becoming a radio psychosexual therapist," he said, ending the silence between them.

"Oh ... that ..." Emem murmured. She paused, sipped from her drink, and then lowered her fork. "I think it started off as rebellion against my family and all the ways I was made to feel like the expelled sinful child of Bishop Akpan."

"Rebellion?" His eyebrows knitted together. "But you're a trained psychologist ... why would your family think anything's wrong with that?"

Bewilderment clouded his eyes.

She shrugged and then leaned forward. "Maybe you'll understand better if I tell you more about my family."

"You don't have to if you—"

Emem smiled, waving a hand to stop him.

"I *do* want to tell you, Yomi." And she meant it.

For the first time ever, someone was showing interest in the reasons for her choices, not judging her, or ignoring her, but actually keen to know. From the way he leaned in, the attentiveness of his gaze, it was obvious.

Nobody, including her best friend Natalie, was privy to the emotional turmoil she'd gone through growing up in a strict religious family. In fact, since her move to Lagos, she'd buried that part of her life deep inside her subconscious, trying hard to forget.

"I grew up in a very religious home," she began, her tone soft and reflective. "When I was younger, I was not allowed to socialise much. I attended a faith-based primary and secondary school, was constantly forced to attend church activities, and had very little experience outside the church."

She drew in a breath, stroking her fingers over the stem of her glass. "As I grew older—my early teens—like normal, I began to have sexual urges that I didn't understand. I remember being very confused. I had hormones raging inside me, but didn't know who to turn to because in my family, nobody talked about such things."

Her stomach churned at the recollection of constantly hearing that sex was a sin, that the desire itself was from the devil, and everyone who so much as entertained the thought without a marriage certificate would be damned to Hell fire. No explanations.

"The first time I asked my father about sex, he took me to the church and forced me to spend the entire day reading a chapter from the Bible until I could recite it word for word by memory. When I missed any word, he would leave me for an hour and come back. I spent a total of eight hours there. I was just thirteen at the time."

His jaw dropped. "That's horrible. No child should have to go through that."

She shook her head, fighting back the painful memory. She hadn't understood what she'd done wrong for asking. She'd just wanted some explanations, some comfort from all the confusion her own sexual awakening had been causing to her mind and body.

"I couldn't talk to my mother, either. She's even worse than my father. She lives in a bubble of spirituality and is always in a trancelike state. The first time I had my period, she handed me some sanitary pads and told me to stay away from boys or I'd die of HIV and go to Hell. That was all she said to me and never spoke of it again."

Yomi shook his head, his face a mask of inner emotions which she couldn't decipher. She wondered briefly if she'd unloaded too much on him, but she couldn't stop the compulsion to let it all out. His interested gaze encouraged her to keep talking.

"So I stopped asking and spent all my teenage years with a rare kind of sexual repressive anxiety. I literally vomited whenever sexually aroused, disgusted with and ashamed of myself."

She paused, afraid that yet again, she'd shared too much information, but his attentive eyes stayed on hers, and his next words reassured her.

"How horrible for you. I never even knew that condition existed. And to be so young going through such ..." He covered her hand with his large hands and squeezed.

"Oh, it does. It's a form of panic attack ... And it was terrible. I couldn't talk to anyone about it. I felt so isolated."

His Adam's apple bobbed as he swallowed hard. "I'm sorry you had to go through that."

"Thanks, Yomi." The heat from his palms comforted and stimulated her at the same time. "My saving grace was my first holiday away from home. I stayed with my maternal grandmother, Ma Josephine." A smile curved her lips at the memory. "I was seventeen years old, and for the first time, my overbearing parents allowed me to follow my grandma back to Calabar. As if Ma Josephine noticed my inner troubles, she insisted I spend an entire month with her, even threatened my father until he agreed."

That had been one of the best holidays of her life. A good listener with a warm personality, her grandmother had been an outlet for all her emotional turmoil.

"When I told Ma Josephine everything, including the anxiety attacks I was having, she introduced me to a trained psychologist who worked in the same university as she did. It took a while, but after a few sessions with Professor Mary Eket of the University of Calabar, my symptoms disappeared, and I could finally feel arousal without vomiting."

"Oh, that's amazing. Is she the one that inspired you—the professor?"

"Yes, and no. At first, I studied psychology because I wanted to be a lecturer like Ma Josephine and Professor Eket. But as the years went by, I noticed the timidity of my younger siblings and realised that they were probably going through the same things I had, but were not bold enough to ask questions."

She pressed her lips into thin lines and straightened her back. All the signs were there. Every time she'd approached her sister or brother, they'd shut her down, calling her the agent of Satan, an evil force. Consequently, she'd simply given up.

"When I wasn't able to support my own siblings because they refused to let me in, I wanted to help others, become an outlet for people scared to talk about sexual difficulties. Discourage the guilt people felt for having sexual desires, especially women who feel ashamed of their sexuality. So, I decided to specialise in Psychosexual Therapy and applied for a Master's degree in Lancashire, England."

Yomi made an approving sound which sent her heart soaring. However, he remained silent, gaze trained on her.

"My parents disapproved vehemently when I got the offer, and despite all the family wealth, they didn't help financially. So, my grandmother stepped in and sponsored me."

"She's cool—Ma Josephine. She must be very proud of you."

"She is ... was." Emem let out a sad sigh. "She died seven years ago."

"Oh, very sorry to hear that."

"No worries. I am okay most of the time. Sometimes, I miss her so much."

Yomi squeezed her hand again and then raised her knuckles to his lips.

"Thanks for telling me this," he whispered as he lowered her hand and picked up his fork. "I read '*Own Your Sexuality*,' and although I loved it, I wish you had included this story."

"You read my book?" She raised a brow in surprise.

"Yes, I'm a huge fan of Sasha the show host and author." He gave her a stunning dimpled grin. "But why do it anonymously? You're doing important work."

She chuckled. "I don't know. My ex ... he was a bit ashamed of my job. I guess it was easier to follow his wishes, because really, anonymity made my job easier. I could say exactly what I felt—what the caller needed to hear—without worrying about people judging me personally."

He nodded as she spoke. "I understand. And Sasha ... how did you come about the name?"

"Simple. I love Beyoncé, her drive and work ethic. I know she has this alter ego—Sasha Fierce—the personality she lets out on stage to be as daring as she wants during her performances. I simply took that idea and name from her."

"Well, anonymous or not, I'm proud of what you are. And I'm honoured to actually know you as Emem as well as Sasha."

"Wow, thank you." She leaned forward and planted a firm kiss on his mouth. "That's the sweetest thing anyone has ever said to me."

The resultant curve of his lips into a sultry smile made her warm and tingly all over.

Oh, my, she mused, staring into Yomi's penetrating dark eyes. *This is getting too intense. Definitely not the casual affair I had in mind.*

CHAPTER TWELVE

Yomi leaned forward and opened the car door on the passenger side. He stepped aside for Emem, who hopped out laughing.

"I swear, Yomi, the dessert wasn't that bad."

"Oh, yes, it was ... Some restaurants should just stick to traditional food only. Worst cheesecake I've ever had," he snorted, also chuckling. "And I should have known better ... Cheese and Nigeria? That's like oil and water. They don't go together."

Her soft laughter trickled down his ears, charging through his veins and culminating in his groin, heightening the sexual awareness that had constantly tormented him all evening, starting from the kiss they'd shared in the theatre. He wanted to throw her over his shoulder, toss her on a bed, and have his way with her. He pushed back that Neanderthal thought and held his hand out to her instead.

"That's not true. I had the best cheese I've ever tasted in my life when I travelled up North," she said, accepting his gesture and strolling hand-in-hand with him into the apartment building entrance.

"Really?" he asked, inserting his key into the lock on the front door.

"Yep, at a small breakfast café in Jos. It was excellent."

"I'll not believe it until I taste it."

"Doubting Thomas ..." she teased, pinching him on his arm playfully.

He snorted out a short laugh as he pushed the door open. "Yes, I am ... seeing is believing. Or in this case, tasting is believing."

Still clasping her hand in his, he escorted her to her apartment entrance. She turned to him at the door and gave him a shy smile which he reflexively returned. Her eyes twinkled as she twirled her finger around the handle of the bag hanging over her shoulder.

"Thanks for a wonderful evening ..." she began, darted her gaze sideways, and then raised her lips to his for a quick kiss. "I enjoyed myself," she murmured, her warm breath against his skin sending a wave of desire spiralling down his body.

His abdominal muscles tightened as she stepped away, and his fingers itched with the desire to pull her back into his space, into his arms, and crush his mouth against hers.

"You're welcome, Emem. I had a great time, too," he said, heart jack-hammering inside his chest as every pore in his body remained aware of her nearness.

They stood facing each other, the air between them thick with uncertainty. Yomi wanted to come in, wanted to make love to her. Badly. All through the drive home, he'd thought about being with her in the most intimate way possible, hoping that his intense attraction to her wasn't one-sided, that she'd invite him in tonight. Even now as he searched her face, it was all he could do not to jump her at the door and press his hard, aroused body against the softness of her curves.

"Eh ... The play was awesome. I'll make sure to leave a review."

Her husky voice cut through his sensual thoughts.

His heart rate amped up. The strong desire to ask if he could come into her apartment warred with his need to be courteous. Although he wanted her physically to the point of distraction, he also wanted a relationship with her, and thus needed to move cautiously so that he didn't destroy any chance of that happening. The thought of scaring her off and losing the ground he'd gained with her caused his stomach to twist. No, he'd rather sleep alone—blue balls, and all— than risk it.

"Yes, excellent idea. I'll do that, too." He cleared his throat which grated from sudden dryness. "We should go out again. Maybe next Saturday?"

"That'd be great," she said.

"Okay, then. See you later, beautiful." Leaning forward, he placed another soft kiss on her mouth and took two steps back.

Fleeting surprise registered in her eyes, before her face became impassive with a blank stare directed at him. Something had flashed in her eyes in the interim. Frustration? Disappointment? Did she also want him to come in?

Before he could voice out his thoughts, she lowered her head and reached into her purse. Averting her gaze from his, she fished out a bunch of keys.

"Okay, see you later."

Deflated, he slumped his shoulders and took two more steps away from her. "I'll call you tomorrow."

"Yes, that would be nice." Her tone sounded strained, her demeanour shuttered.

Lingering for seconds, he wondered what he'd done wrong. Whether he should just bite the bullet and ask her if he could spend the night. If she turned him down, he'd know she wasn't ready, and he was okay with waiting. But what if she wanted him to make love to her tonight, explore the chemistry that sizzled between them all evening? Would she push him away if he pulled her towards him and pressed her against his body?

Her words interrupted his reveries before he had a chance to fish for answers to those questions.

"I've got to pee," she mumbled, turning to the door and unlocking it. "Talk to you tomorrow."

"Bright and early," he said, waving a hand as she dashed into her apartment and shut the door.

Bright and early... how dumb.

"Who in the world says bright and early?" he muttered to himself as he stood there feeling awkward, and sensing he'd just messed up.

There was something that he'd misinterpreted or missed from her initial expression, which had made her withdraw into herself, and he wanted to kick himself in the shin for that inexperienced blunder. He'd always assumed he could read women. At least, with his three exes, he'd been able to piece together their inaudible communications and deduce their mood. But his fear of losing Emem had made him doubt himself.

Major F-up, idiot. Raking a palm down his face, he shook his head as a realisation hit him. Emem had wanted him to come in, to make the first move, and now, the moment was gone.

Well, he'd just have to be patient, he thought as he strolled towards the stairway. For him, this wasn't only about sex. He wanted Emem's body, no doubt. But he also wanted all of her, her friendship, her intelligence, even her baggage. Everything. It had to be an all-inclusive package for him, and he wouldn't be satisfied with anything less. He'd wait for her until he could be guaranteed that.

***

I've got to pee ... how stupid!

Emem shook her head as she rested her back against the closed door. She placed a palm over her chest in a feeble attempt to control the vibrations of her pounding heart.

"Huge mess up," she groaned, grimacing with mortification as she tried to curtail her disappointment.

Why couldn't a grown woman like herself make the first move, ask a man she found insanely attractive to come inside her apartment and make love to her? Considering that was essentially what had occupied her thoughts all evening.

After the kiss they'd shared at the theatre and then throughout dinner, even when she'd been baring her soul to him, it had taken almost superhuman effort not to blurt out how she wanted the night to end. With him on top of her, under her, whatever position, as long as she could feel him inside her, all over her.

It was strange, this reckless desire for a man she hardly knew. Yet, she couldn't seem to control it. His tall, athletic build, the masculinity that oozed from him, his scent, those dangerous dimples, and most of all, his laid-back personality, made it all the more difficult to resist his allure. And she knew he felt some attraction to her; she could see it in his eyes. Why hadn't he pushed for sex tonight? Was he being chivalrous? Trying to take things slow like she'd requested?

Oh, how she wished she'd never said that. Her body hummed with a strong desire to go knocking on his door and making it clear that slow wasn't what she needed at the moment. She wanted *fast*, *hard*, him with her, inside her, tonight. Not tomorrow.

Scrubbing a palm down her face, she shook her head again. She wasn't that bold, and she knew it. She'd chickened out at the door, and now, the opportunity was lost. Such a wonder how she could be so daring when telling others to take control of their sexuality on the radio and in her book, but couldn't heed her own advice.

Shoulders drooping with disappointment, she jerked away from the door and strolled to her room. She dumped her bag unceremoniously onto the dressing table and slumped on the bed.

Lying in the dark, she replayed the evening in her head, reliving the sweet moments of Yomi holding her, smiling at her, showing concern when she'd told him about her family. All evening, he'd touched her skin at various intervals with a welcomed familiarity that loving couples shared, igniting her blood with each tactile motion.

Then, her thoughts drifted to the memory of their kiss in the theatre, the slow but erotic stroke of his tongue inside her mouth, the deep and low groans he'd made, and her body flooded with heat, moist pleasure tightening the nub between her thighs.

Spreading them wider apart, she dragged her hand down her body and slid a finger under her dress. She shut her eyes and concentrated on the image of a bare-chested Yomi forming at the back of her mind, trying to visualise the hard planes of his chest, his strong arms and the calligraphy inked on them. He'd told her what the tattoos meant. On one arm was the large symbol of *loyalty*, and on the other, *family*. All in black traditional Chinese characters that she itched to trace with her tongue.

Moisture pooled at the crotch of her panties at the sensual picture. Her mouth parted into a soft moan as she brushed her finger over her throbbing centre. Getting more worked up, she slipped her finger under her panties, and just as she guided it inside her sleek vagina, a loud, lyrical sound jarred her from the carnal act.

Snapping her eyes open and snatching her hand away from underneath her dress, Emem jumped from the bed. She rushed to her dressing table and zipped open her handbag.

Frantically, she rummaged inside for her phone, hoping that it was Yomi calling to ask if he could come over tonight to put an end to the sexual tension coiling inside her belly.

"Shit," she cursed when she retrieved it and glanced at the screen. *If only wishes were horses.*

She slid a thumb across the phone screen and anchored it against her ear with her shoulder whilst rubbing her finger over a wet wipe she'd pulled out from a packet on the table.

"How was your date with Mr. *Oyibo*?" Natalie's jovial voice reverberated from the other end of the line.

"Don't. He doesn't like being called that—that and JJC."

"Hmm ... Someone is getting to know Mr. *Oyibo* ... ehm ...Yomi, better."

"Shut up, girl."

"So ..."

"So, what?"

"How was the date with Yomi?"

Emem sank into the seat in front of the mirror and tossed the wipe into the small bin on the floor beside her.

"It was wonderful. The play was amazing. You should see it, too. It runs every week until the end of this month—"

"Focus, babe, or I'll kill you." Natalie's rumbustious voice cut her off. "The important details first. Number one: Did you guys kiss? Number two: Do you like him?"

A smile pulled the corner of Emem's lips upwards. "Yes, we did. And yes, I do."

Natalie's squeal of delight in her ear widened her smile.

"Girl! That's fantastic. You need a new man. Best way to get over a man is to get under another one."

"Be serious!"

"I am, and I mean it, Emem. Sometimes, a relationship isn't supposed to lead to anything. Just like you don't buy every car you test-drive. Just go with the flow, girl."

"I'm going with the flow."

"No, you're not. I've known you for five years. You talk a good game on your radio show, but you never let yourself live. For once, don't allow your self-imposed limitations to hold you back. Be Emem. Be happy."

"I *am* being Emem."

"Again, no, you're not. I know that, and that's why I called you at this time of the night not worried about interrupting anything."

"What do you mean?"

"Why are you on the phone talking to me and not under Yomi like you want to be? Why did you stop yourself from going for what you want tonight?"

Flabbergasted that Natalie had hit the nail right on the head, Emem had no response.

"Darling, I read your book, and it changed me. Use your own words as wings and soar, baby, soar. You owe it to yourself."

Emem sucked her lower lip into her mouth as she listened. Indeed, she'd written a whole chapter titled *Making the First Move*, encouraging women not to worry about being seen as aggressive, or being labelled a slut, or even concern themselves with opinions other than what they felt. The last two sentences of that chapter jumped to her mind.

'Finally, be good to yourself. Besides, how will you know if you don't try?'

Chapter Thirteen

Sleep eluded Yomi as he lay on his back atop the silky bedspread of his king-sized bed. He picked up his mobile phone and glanced at the screen. Twelve-o-four a.m.

Switching on the bedside lamp, he pulled himself slightly upright, resting his head against the bedpost.

He scrolled to Emem's contact number and pressed on the screen.

'I enjoyed myself on our date. I am awake and thinking about you. Actually, I'm not only thinking, I'm yearning for you, to touch you'

"No, sounds too needy," he muttered to himself in frustration. He pressed the backspace button and deleted the last sentence. Tapping rapidly on his mobile device, he continued.

'Actually, I'm not only thinking about you, I'm longing to be with you tonight ...'

"Too poetic!" he grunted, tossing his phone on the side of the bed and abandoning the fifth attempted text message to Emem since he had left her at the door of her apartment.

What the hell was wrong with him? He'd never felt so uncertain in his life, so restless. And he'd never wanted a woman so badly that it interfered with his sleep. He'd immediately taken a cold shower when he'd gotten back to his apartment, hoping it would help.

It hadn't. Instead, he had replayed the entire day over and over again in his mind. Images of Emem in the gown that accentuated her generous curves, her smile, her soft lips pressed against him, and those throaty moans that had escaped her lips when they'd kissed had constantly plagued his heightened senses.

For the past hour, his penis had kept rising and falling at intervals, keeping him awake and horny, until he'd decided to accept that he wouldn't get any shut eye tonight.

He sighed as he glanced down at the semi-erection tenting his pyjama bottoms. Maybe he should just take matters into his own hands.

He shook his head. That wouldn't be enough. Ever. Not when he'd already had a taste of the sweetness of her mouth. No. He'd never be able to get close to the satisfaction he craved by touching himself. Nothing but the contact of her flesh with his would do.

A sudden flashing of his phone alerted him. Startled, he reached for it, almost dropping it in his haste.

He glanced at the screen and froze. A picture message from Emem. All the blood in his brain drained south and hardened his penis further until he felt it would slice through the fabric of his clothing as his eyes widened at the image on display—Emem with a black scarf covering her face, but clad in a lacy red lingerie, body stretched across the bed at a sexy angle.

Spellbound, he stared at the erotic image of her glorious ebony skin glowing in the reflection from the light and her barely covered bottom inclined at the camera.

His phone chimed again with another text message, breaking his trance.

With shaky fingers, he scrolled to the WhatsApp message under the picture.

'I'm deleting this photo in 5 mins. I want you over in my room in less.'

Quickly overcoming his inertness, he sprang up from the bed. Heart racing like a speedboat, he peeled off his clothes and changed hastily into a pair of khaki shorts and the nearest plain T-shirt hanging on the door of his wardrobe.

He grabbed his phone from the bed and peeked at the screen. Emem's sexy picture still graced the display—a few more seconds to spare.

Rushing to the bathroom, he switched on the light. He removed the scarf over his head and ran his fingers through his locks to loosen them, and then lifted a bottle of mouthwash from the sink base. He swirled a capful of the minty liquid inside his mouth and spat it out. After a final glimpse at his reflection in the mirror, he reached for the box of condoms in the vanity cabinet attached to the wall.

Inserting three packets in his pocket, he raced out of the room just as the picture message disappeared from the screen.

Jumping down each flight of stairs, he dashed to Emem's front door and tapped softly. No response after a few seconds. He tapped again, chest heaving and stomach churning, worried he'd not gotten here fast enough.

Just as he reached into his pocket to retrieve his phone, the door opened wide. His body became immobilised, and his manhood rose in immediate salute to the beauty that greeted his eyes.

With a sultry smile on her lips, Emem stood in front of him, covered in a pink dressing gown belted at her narrow waist, bringing his focus to her perfect hourglass figure. He couldn't prevent his eyes from trailing over her body, or his hands from reaching out to pull her to him for a hug.

"I want you so bloody much," he rasped when she flung her arms around his neck, drawing him closer, her flowery scent enveloping him.

"Me, too, Yomi. I want you, too."

Trembling all over, he held onto her, basking in the rightness of her in his arms, relishing the perfect fit of her softness against his hard, aroused body.

"We ... we should go in."

Her husky voice penetrated his thoughts.

"Yes, we should," he said, his voice terse and unrecognisable from the thick desire clogging his throat. "I don't want an audience for what I want to do to you."

She giggled softly in response as she pulled him into her apartment and shut the door—a sensual sound that sent waves of desire charging through him, making him feel a bit giddy.

"Would you like to eat or drink anything first?"

Her polite question produced a bark of laughter from deep within his belly.

"What? I want to feed you before I use up all your energy," she said, eyes twinkling, her mischievous candour turning him on all the more.

"You," he answered, pulling her back into his arms. "I want to eat and drink you 'til morning."

He brought his mouth down on hers for a searing wet kiss. Groaning at the pleasurable sensation of the contact of her tongue with his, he pulled her closer, stroking her back with his large hands.

The soft moan from her lips as her hands draped over his neck shot straight to his groin, stretching his manhood impossibly longer, making him want to toss her on the couch and take her hard and fast with no decorum.

Breaking contact with her to tamp down the heat flooding his senses, he whispered, "Your room."

A smile curved her lips as she held her hand out to him. Yomi took the delicate palm in his and followed her lead across the sitting room and down a short corridor.

She pushed open the door to a moderate-sized but elegantly decorated room with a large bed at the centre. He focused on the pristine beige-coloured bedcover draping the wooden bed.

"Freshly laundered sheets," he murmured, inhaling deeply. "Did you plan this for me, beautiful?"

She gave him a shy smile before nodding. "Yes, handsome. I changed the sheets this morning, hoping our date would end here."

Her sincere response held him still. The fact that she'd wanted him from the beginning of the day aroused him to an almost unbearable point.

"Oh, baby," he rasped, hauling her into his arms.

Without any more words needed, he lowered his head and recaptured her mouth in his, hands clutching the short coils that crowned her head as he drew her closer. He couldn't get enough of the taste of her mouth, the hot sweetness of pleasure the confident strokes of her tongue sparked in him.

"Emem ... oh, God," he groaned, dragging his hand down her perfectly carved skull, over her back, and cupping her bottom through her gown.

The softness against his palm sent a jolt of arousal down his spine, concentrating in his penis. He squeezed both butt cheeks firmly, grinding her pelvis over the straining bulge in his shorts, trying to sooth the fire burning in his loins.

"Yomi," she cried out, reaching in-between them to grasp his engorged manhood in her soft palms. "Make love to me now, please."

Her husky plea drummed in his brain, making him lose his mind with the intensity of the need erupting in his veins.

Letting out a guttural moan, he drew back and unfastened the belt of her dressing gown, pulling it over her shoulders and watching as it fell in a puddle at her ankles.

He swept his gaze hungrily over the sexy lace bra pushing large breasts upwards. The erotic image before him knocked the breath out of his lungs, and he parted his mouth to recapture his breath.

"You're fucking sexy, Emem," he groaned, cupping her lace-covered breasts. "I'm not sure if I want to leave this on or take it off."

"Off, please," she whispered, turning her back to him. "I want no clothes between us."

His gaze dropped to her bottom and the scanty lace over the perfectly rounded globes of flesh jutting towards him, demanding to be noticed. He halted for seconds, confused about what to focus his attention on—unclasping her bra, or touching the glorious nearly-naked ass before him.

"Like what you see back there?"

Her audacious question snapped him out of his transfixed fascination.

"Oh ... yes ... so bloody much..."

"Thank you, handsome, but there's enough time to look later, you know. I want you now."

"Lord have mercy," he growled as he unclasped her bra with shaky fingers.

Eyes burning with lust, he watched as Emem turned towards him and swiftly slid her panties down her thick, firm thighs.

He stood motionless, captivated by her beautiful large breasts, turgid dark nipples pointing upwards, begging for his hungry mouth, the slenderness of her waist which tapered into round, shapely hips. The definition of perfection.

And goodness, a shiny belly button ring gleamed at the centre of her flat stomach, the sexy silver stud so arousing that his balls tightened, threatening to discharge all its contents onto his shorts before they'd even started.

"Oh, God, Emem, you're ... stunning, man," he groaned, reaching for her with eager hands, his practiced Nigerian accent completely gone, giving way to the unguarded cockney dialect of East End Londoners.

She held his arm to stop him.

"Nope, there'll be plenty of time for nice and slow ..." she whispered, walking over to the bed, her round bottom jiggling as she moved. She sat down, reached under the pillow, and pulled out a packet of condoms. "Plenty ... But now, I want it hard and rough."

"Oh ... Emem!" Yomi rasped, dragging his shirt over his shoulders rapidly and pulling down his shorts in one quick move. "You're playing with fire ..."

Her soft giggle fuelled his arousal as he rushed to the bed and jumped onto it beside her.

*

Emem's laughter quickly died off, replaced with sharp moans of pleasure as Yomi covered her body with his, trailing kisses over her neck, and then her breasts, suckling, licking and nicking both with fervour.

"Oh ... Yomi ..." she whimpered when he gathered her breasts together in his palms, feasting his wet mouth on them almost simultaneously, his deep hums of satisfaction devastatingly arousing.

"You have the loveliest nipples, so dark and large ..." he murmured, tugging one swollen bud with his teeth gently. "I can't get enough of them ... of you ..."

A rush of moist pleasure gushed from her core, making her squirm. She wanted him inside her now, the foreplay not needed.

"Yomi ..." she pleaded, parting her thighs wider and shoving her hips upwards. "Now ... please ..."

"Not yet, baby ... I want you to scream by the time I slide inside ..." He dragged his palm down her stomach and twirled his finger over her belly button, his eyes dark and intense. "This is so sexy ..."

His raw compliment was quickly followed by the swirl of his tongue over the silver stud that pierced her skin. Emem curved her back off the bed, the image of his long pink tongue working its magic on her belly almost sending her over the edge.

"Yomi ... now!" she ordered, grabbing a fistful of his locks and yanking it.

A loud growl of pain tore from him, and then, his prolonged sigh of pleasure reverberated in the room as he spread her legs wider apart.

"I'm going to make you scream," he declared in a raw voice, sinking his teeth into the fleshy skin of her inner thigh.

Painful pleasure shot directly to her throbbing core, tightening the nub nestled there.

"Yomi!" she screeched as tiny spasms clenched her vagina.

"Yes, Emem ... that's my bloody name," he grunted.

Without giving her a second to catch her breath, he swiped his tongue over the sore area, and almost immediately after, over her clit.

"Ahhh ..." she gasped, eyes rolling shut, thrashing her head from side to side, unable to believe the intensity of pleasure that gripped her entire body from the stroke of his wicked tongue.

Expertly, he feasted between her thighs, driving her mad with need, her body quaking, clenched fists clutching his locks as she pressed her wet mound against his face.

"Don't stop ... please don't stop," she moaned, feeling a strong climax building up from deep within her core.

She felt his finger inside her just as he sucked her swollen nub into his mouth.

"Yomi!"

A shrill cry erupted from her as an intense release rippled through her body, curling her toes and squeezing the breath out of her lungs.

Dazed and motionless from the force of her climax, she watched as he sheathed his engorged shaft with a condom, the thick meat jutting from his body and curving towards her, like a weapon set for battle.

Her throat went dry at the size of his erection. Why on Earth had she dismissed him as a younger man? Gosh, he was built like a horse, a magnificent male beast made to bring satisfaction to any female ...

His deep groan as he flipped her on her stomach and pulled her towards the edge of the bed interrupted her train of thought.

He clutched a handful of her ass and let out a harsh growl. "These right here ..." he rasped as he swatted her left butt cheek with his palm, and then the right. "Perfect ... round ... soft ... mine ..."

The sharp stings of his palm swiping her bottom with each word he uttered ignited a ball of fire in her loins, making her whimper from pain and pleasure, the sensations almost indistinguishable and unbelievably erotic.

Curving her back further and pushing her bottom upwards in offering to him, she moaned.

"Now ... please ..." Her face pressed onto the mattress muffled her plea.

"Please, what, Emem? Please stop ... please don't ..."

"Please fuck me, make me come again..."

"Okay, then, darling. Your wish is my command."

Profound ecstasy sliced through her at the sensation of his thick manhood filling her with a confident thrust.

"Oh, God!" she cried out, eyes rolling shut, mouth wide open.

"Yes! Yes!" he groaned as he plunged in and out of her with long, sure strokes that hit all her nerve endings repeatedly, and at the right pace. His fingers moved downwards and squeezed her clit.

She screamed, an incoherent and carnal sound.

"I wish you could see how perfectly we fit together, baby, how well your sweet pussy is swallowing my dick."

His gruff words, the fervent piston-like movement of his shaft inside her vagina, the exquisite sensation of his fingers stroking her clit, all combined, hit her with an unexpected climax that slammed into her with force.

"Oooooh!" she yelled, squeezing her eyes tight as her body shuddered violently in helpless surrender to an abyss of intense sensual gratification.

Sounds of body slapping against body filled the air as Yomi quickened his pace behind her, his moans of pleasure harsher, prolonging her own orgasm.

Six more thrusts, and his body tensed before he jerked his own release, a guttural shout from him echoing in her ears.

"God! Emem," he gasped as he collapsed on her back. "You're incredible ..."

Blissfully sated, she closed her eyes, enjoying the pressure of his weight and the warmth of his slick body on top of her.

"Oh, you did all the work this time ... all the credit goes to you, baby," she purred, still tingling from the aftershocks of her breath-taking climax.

CHAPTER FOURTEEN

Emem peeled her eyes open and rolled to her side, stretching her arm across the bed. Empty. She sat upright and stilled at the complete silence of the room, wondering whether Yomi had gone back to his flat. Then, his soft, melodious whistle floated into her ears from the sitting room. A slow smile stretched her lips.

He must be busy with his obsessive Sunday morning cleaning of her apartment. Although she'd told him many times not to, he couldn't seem to function in a less than flawlessly organised space. And she'd decided not to stop him. It didn't hurt anyone, and it certainly made her flat tidier. A win-win situation.

Her smile widened as she thought about last night, an enjoyable evening spent dancing in a reggae club which had ended on this bed in a marathon of sexual pleasure for both of them.

Sighing with happiness, she curved her back like a satiated cat. She could get used to this, waking up sated to the clatter of a stunning man cleaning her flat.

Since their first date four weeks ago, she and Yomi had shared many stimulating phone conversations, humorous text messages, exciting date nights, and satisfying sexual encounters.

Not only did their chemistry between the sheets sizzle, they also shared a connection which she'd never found with anyone else. His sense of humour aligned with hers so much that they'd burst into laughter several times at one odd observation or another without any words needed between them.

Just like two days ago, while seated at the balcony of his apartment, they'd spotted a woman passing by in the street, holding a goat under her arm like it was a handbag.

They had both exchanged a shocked glance and erupted into prolonged giggles, almost falling out of their seats. She hadn't even needed to ask Yomi why that had amused him; he'd simply echoed her thoughts about the idea of a goat-shaped purse being a possible fashion hit.

Yomi got her. And that felt good. The mere thought of him always made her giddy with happiness, and she couldn't help herself from free-floating into the idea of them as a couple. Which she shouldn't, really, given that he would eventually want something she couldn't give him. Not naturally, anyway.

Shaking her head to clear it from that gloomy thought, she rose from the bed and pulled down the silk nightgown bunched on her upper thigh. As she took a step towards the bathroom, a mild discomfort pulsed at the flesh between her thighs.

"Mmmm," she moaned, halting abruptly.

Standing still, she clenched the muscles of her inner walls, breathing out slowly through her mouth. It was always a pleasure being pummelled into blissful oblivion by Yomi's thick and long dick. But she eventually paid for it the morning after with sore muscles everywhere in her body.

She shook her head, her lips still curved into a smile at the memory of how seconds after unlocking the door to her apartment last night, they'd pounced on each other on the floor of the sitting room, and then on the wall of the bedroom before finally making it to the bed.

His stamina amazed her. She'd never experienced repeated multiple orgasms with either of her two exes.

In fact, Ejike had been a selfish lover, and she'd had to finish off by herself many times.

But Yomi seemed able to keep going with almost superhuman effort that left her feeling thoroughly satisfied and exhausted at the same time. She wasn't complaining, though. As long as he continued to bring her pleasure with his meaty organ and long tongue, she'd put up with just a bit of soreness down below.

Chuckling at her naughtiness, she sauntered to the bathroom and quickly cleaned her teeth. Ten minutes later, she strolled into her sitting room to find a shirtless Yomi bowed over an opened cardboard box, transferring books from it onto the wooden bookshelf under the flat screen television.

She took a moment to admire him while he was distracted, his eyes concentrating on a book in his hand.

Such a stunning male. His long locks, let loose, fell down his shoulders, caressing the upper part of a lithe back with no love-handles whatsoever in sight.

With his shorts hanging low on his hips, a fraction of his butt-crack gaped through, revealing a bit of what she knew lay between a firm, tight ass. Sparse curly hairs covered his chest, which gave him a sexy, masculine look. Indeed, she couldn't get enough of feeling the silky curls sliding through her fingers whenever she ran her palms down his chest and over his firm abdomen. Gosh, watching him made her core moisten again.

"Kama Sutra for disabled couples?"

Yomi's deep voice broke through her errant scrutiny.

"Wh-What?" she sputtered, confused at first about his remark until she saw the book in his hand. "Oh ..."

She moved farther into the room.

"Yes, oh," he quipped, eyes brimming with amusement. "In all my years, I've never ever considered this issue before now."

She laughed out. "It was a research topic for my Master's—sexual fulfilment in disabled couples. I had to interview amputees, people with various congenital defects and other physical disabilities. It was interesting to find out that sexual desires and fulfilment for them was just the same as for those without any physical challenges. Only harder to attain."

"Hmm ... I learn new things from you every day, babe."

Seconds of silence followed as she joined him on the floor and pulled a book from the box.

"You don't have to unpack for me, you know. I'll do it sometime later."

"I really don't mind, Emem." He flashed her a charming smile. "I enjoy organising stuff. Helps clear my head. Besides, I didn't want to wake you."

Leaning forward, she pressed her lips to his forehead with a quick kiss. "Thanks, I'll join you for a bit." As an afterthought, she asked, "Have you eaten breakfast yet? I could fry some plantains ..."

"Yes, I had some cornflakes."

"That's not a proper breakfast."

"Trust me, it was. My bowl was so full that it almost spilled over."

She chuckled. "You like cereals too much."

"And you rarely eat breakfast."

"I used to ... It's just that with us eating late almost every night for the past four weeks, I feel myself putting on weight. So, skipping breakfast is my way of ..."

"Stop it. You're perfect." He tilted her face up with his thumb and forefinger, an intense spark in his

117

dark eyes. "Absolutely P.E.R.F.E.C.T," he murmured, reciting each letter with soft kisses on her mouth.

The rawness of his tone made her head spin, and the tenderness of his gaze caused her throat to tighten with tears. As she stared deep into his eyes, she realised that without putting up much of a fight, she had fallen in love with him.

The realisation made her heart ache. This wasn't the plan. She was supposed to have a light fling with him. Enjoy a free-spirited affair, not fall for a man she would eventually end up hurting.

Rising abruptly, she turned towards the kitchen. "I need to get some tea."

He rose, too, and grabbed her arm, forcing her to face him.

"I'm moving too fast for you, aren't I?" he asked, his voice thick with anxiety.

"No ... I, eh ..."

"Then why did you just freeze up on me?"

"I didn't."

He shrugged, sucked his teeth, and then stepped right in front of her. The invasion of her personal space was both threatening and exciting at the same time. An utterly complex emotion, because from the clenching of his jaw muscles, she knew he was about to tell her exactly what had been occupying his mind while he'd been helping her unpack her boxes.

"I want you to meet my family."

His request was met with startled silence. Unable to respond, she simply stared at him, frozen to the spot.

That didn't seem to deter him. He brushed his thumb across her cheek in a soft caress.

"My father is planning an intimate gathering at our family home for my thirtieth birthday celebration in two weeks. I want you to be there with me."

Still silence.

"As my girlfriend."

She wanted this, too. To be his girlfriend. Even more. But that would be selfish. He deserved a younger woman, and a woman who would fulfil his every dream. She couldn't allow Yomi to tie himself down to her. When she knew how much that would eventually hurt him. No, she needed to stop this emotional pull between them, make him believe that their liaison only involved sex.

She should have tried harder to keep the boundaries clear. But it had been difficult because of the way she felt about him, the powerful attraction to him that she'd never experienced with any other man.

"We've only been together for four weeks ..." she began weakly.

"Bullshit," he cut her off. "That's an excuse. Not buying it. What's the issue? The real issue. And please don't tell me it's our age difference."

Emem hesitated, the desire to break down and reveal the shameful truth about her own physical handicap rising to the tip of her tongue. However, she stopped herself from spilling her guts. She just couldn't tell him. Not ever. Better to end their relationship now.

"Well, we aren't exactly a normal match. Don't you think your family would be surprised when you bring home a woman nearly ten years older than you to dinner?"

"Oh, yes, they would."

"You see, I'm right—"

"Not because of your age or mine, or any of that nonsense. But because this would be the first time I'd be bringing a woman home for dinner."

She became still. That couldn't be true, could it? "Now, you're lying ..."

"Don't insult me. I don't need to lie to you about anything."

"Then be honest, admit it. I'm too old for you. Be honest about the fact that it would never work between us."

"I'll admit nothing," he ground out through clenched teeth, the muscles at the side of his temples bunched up as a slow flush crept up his neck. "You and I know that the age difference between us is insignificant. As a matter of fact, I remember you yelling out 'give it to me, Daddy! Yes, Daddy,' more times than I could count last night. Am I really too young for you, or do you go about calling all younger men *Daddy*?"

A shocked gasp gushed from her parted lips.

"Oh, how mature! Using my sexual vulnerability to attack me," she retorted, her angry bark a thick spear that sliced the tension in the air.

The room fell silent, Yomi's heaving breath the only distinct sound in the room, the tendons of his neck straining as though from the effort of fighting to regain control of his emotions.

"Emem," he said finally, his tone gentler. "I'm falling in love with you. This is not a game for me. I'm not experimenting. I want us to be together as a couple. And I sense you want the same."

He paused, reaching out to cradle her face in his large hands.

"Deal with whatever issues you have in your head preventing you from letting me in here." He touched the left side of her chest with his finger. "With or without me, resolve that shit, because my intentions are very clear. I won't be your booty call, won't accept anything less than a real attempt at a relationship with you."

He released her and took a step back. "I'm leaving for my apartment."

"Yomi ..."

"No, Emem. If we aren't a couple, we can't be friends. And certainly not friends with benefits. The way I feel about you won't permit that."

"Yomi, I ..."

He leaned forward and brushed a kiss on her lips.

"When you make up your mind about what you want, you know where to find me."

With that final statement, he strolled over to the corner of the room, snatched his shirt off the sofa, and exited her apartment without a backward glance, leaving her staring at the closed door, a hole burning in her devastated heart.

CHAPTER FIFTEEN

Eyes fixed on the computer screen in front of him, Yomi could see nothing. He'd just read the congratulatory email from the members of the board to him about winning the pitch for the Imo State recreational park he'd designed singlehandedly, yet he couldn't seem to share in the jubilation with everyone else in the firm.

Even the ten percent bonus increase he'd receive as a result didn't excite him. All he could think about as he sat in his office fiddling idly with the keyboard was how much he missed Emem, how badly he wanted to share this good news with her.

Five days. It had been five whole days, and he had not heard from her. Not seen her, or even caught a glimpse of her in their building.

Worried about bumping into her on his way to and from the apartment or in the compound, he'd been leaving for work as early as five in the morning and coming back home way after midnight.

He couldn't face her just yet, knowing all the defences he'd built to maintain his distance would crumble at the sight of her lovely face. He'd only give in and accept whatever terms she dealt him, as long as they were together.

But he couldn't. He wouldn't cheapen the way he felt about her by agreeing to be her booty-call neighbour.

For the four weeks they'd been dating, he'd begun to sense her holding back a part of herself from him. Not sexually, but emotionally. There were little pointers that he'd noticed, like the way she closed up when he wanted to talk about the future, swiftly changing the topic, or whenever she made a joke anytime he expressed deeper non-sexual emotions.

To test his suspicion, he'd deliberately declined sex with her after a night out three days before their argument. She'd immediately scrambled out of his apartment, refusing to spend the night in his bed or even stay back to hang out. That night, he'd realised Emem's intentions—to box him out of her emotional space, set some form of boundaries to make it clear she didn't see a future with him. And she'd proven it three days later by shutting him out when he'd invited her to meet his family.

That hurt like hell. Because he was already head over heels in love with her. Without a doubt. Maybe even before he'd met her. All he could think about was having Emem in his life forever. He'd even begun to have images of her and him having a small family of their own. Getting married, or moving in together if she preferred, as long as she was his.

The idea of being her husband appealed to him so much that he'd begun combing through the Internet for engagement rings, going through real estate websites, searching for affordable family homes he could mortgage for them. And to his embarrassment, he'd seen a baby a week ago and immediately thought about what their children would look like. Ruminations he'd never had with any woman he'd met before her.

Yes, he admitted it all seemed too soon and intense, but he couldn't control how deeply rooted his feelings for her had become. He knew with utmost conviction that it didn't make a difference if he'd met her only six weeks ago or millions of years prior—the fact remained that he wanted a future with her by his side. And not just a fleeting one.

Yomi sighed as he moved the desktop mouse around the table, clicking on the 'close' button to log off his email. A thick band of tension tightened the muscles between his shoulder blades as his eyes caught the date on the edge of the computer screen, and he massaged his neck attempting to ease some of it.

Friday. Although he was glad the week had rolled by quickly, tonight, Sasha would be on air, and he wasn't sure he could cope with hearing Emem's voice, knowing she wasn't in his life anymore.

Had he messed up by giving her an ultimatum? Had he been too hasty? What if she'd replaced him with another man? A man who didn't give ultimatums and accepted whatever type of arrangement she needed.

He shook his head. No, he didn't want to think he could be so easily replaced. He and Emem had shared something special these past few weeks. And he knew with certainty that she also felt something for him. So, why hadn't she come to seek him out? Why was she deliberately trying to push him away?

He'd been on the Internet researching her family, scrutinising her social media accounts. Nothing extraordinary had jumped out from his search. No ex-husband or boyfriend drama. No grotesque family secrets. Nothing.

Apart from finding that her family owned a successful religious dynasty, they were all pretty much scandal-free. Even Emem's social media presence was minimal, with only a few random pictures of her on Instagram and Facebook.

So, he couldn't guess why she was so nervous about being with him. He didn't believe for one minute that their age difference had anything to do with it. Unless, maybe she just didn't feel anything but sexual attraction for him.

Heaving a frustrated sigh, he halted that depressing thought. He needed to talk to someone about all this. Only one person came to mind.

Rising to his feet, he lifted his mobile phone from his desk, scrolled through his directory, and dialled a number. It rang three times before the line connected.

"Hello, Segun. Are you in your office?" he asked his brother.

"Yup, been here all day," Segun's voice rang out cheerfully. "Everything okay?" he queried, a worried lilt slipping into his tone.

"Yes, I'm fine," Yomi assured quickly. "Are you busy? I'd like to drop by your office."

"Not at all, you can come by now. I was just about to have a cuppa. Should I make one for you?"

"Perfect, bro. See you in a bit."

"See you soon."

Yomi inserted his phone into his black trousers after ending the call and strolled out of his office, locking the door behind him.

The soles of his black leather shoes tapped heavily on the wooden floorboards as he strode down the hallway and to his brother's office.

"Come in," Segun called out just as he raised his hand to knock.

Yomi twisted his lips into a smirk. Damn his noisy shoes. He could never sneak up on anyone on this floor.

"Hey, bro." He stepped into the large, sparsely decorated workspace. Minimalism and practicality— typical of his brother's penchant for simplicity.

Segun rose from behind his desk, a bright smile on his face as he walked over and pulled him into a hearty hug, tapping his back. "Hey, mate, you've been scarce. I've not seen you for weeks."

Yomi smiled as he followed his brother back to the desk and pulled out a seat. It always amused him that

125

despite ten years of living in Nigeria, Segun's British accent was still as thick as ever.

"I've been occupied," he replied, sinking into the plush leather cushion in front of the desk.

"With what?"

"Nothing, really ... Well, that's what I came to talk to you about."

Segun strolled back behind the desk and lifted a small kettle from the mobile kitchen beside him. "Tea?"

Yomi nodded. "Yes, thanks."

He watched as his brother filled both teacups and shook his head when Segun pointed at the sugar pack on the tray. He lifted his cup to his lips, took a sip, and sighed with pleasure. "Nothing like a good old cuppa."

"Totally agree, mate," Segun said, lowering himself into his executive leather seat. "One of the things I miss about Oxford. Tea breaks with the laddies."

Yomi laughed. "Can't relate, matie. Not at University of Kent. Lager breaks were our thing."

Segun's face stretched into an amused smirk.

"True ... true." He sipped his tea silently for a few seconds. "So, what's going on? Why did you want to see me?"

Yomi lowered his teacup onto the saucer on the dark pine desk in front of him. He leaned back onto his seat.

"I'm seeing someone ... *was* seeing someone, and I'm in love with her."

"Wait, what? When did this happen? We had dinner with Kunle and Dad just two months ago ..."

The shock registering on Segun's face gave Yomi pause. If his brother looked this astonished, he'd definitely been moving too fast with Emem. And she most definitely had reacted to his proposal about meeting his family appropriately.

"I met her about six weeks ago."

"And you're in love?"

"Well ... yes. I can explain it. She's amazing. Funny, beautiful, intelligent. And most importantly, we vibe. She gets me."

His vehement response seemed to startle Segun into prolonged silence. Yomi watched as his brother drank his tea with concentration, eyebrows angled together.

"I understand. I fell for Miriam the first time I saw her. Even then, I knew she was the one," Segun finally said, breaking the silence. His voice held a melancholic lilt that Yomi couldn't ignore.

"What's up, bro?" he asked, noticing the dark bags under Segun's eyes for the first time since he'd walked into the room.

Segun shook his head and forced a stiff smile. "No, we're here to talk about you ..."

"I know, but something's also up with you. Are you okay? Miriam? The girls?"

Segun's Adam's apple bobbed as he swallowed hard. "Miriam filed for a divorce two days ago. I'm staying at Dad's in the meantime."

His breath hitched, astonishment making his chest close up. This unexpected announcement from his brother took him by surprise. He'd been the one who had helped Segun to move back home with Miriam nearly three months ago. They'd looked so happy together, and Yomi had assumed their relationship was on the mend.

"Wow ... I can't believe it. I thought you guys were working things out ..."

"We were ... but I hurt her deeply. And I think I've lost her for good now."

"Oh, man, I had no clue. I'm sorry, Segun. Here I am bugging you with my own shit when you're—"

His brother waved a hand to stop him. "Please, let's talk about what you came here for. I need to think about something other than my failed marriage. I need that, Yomi."

Yomi gave Segun a sympathetic look. "It will be okay. It has to be. You and Miriam were made for each other."

"I know. I'll forever love her. But she deserves to be happy. I can't keep trying to hold onto her when she wants to leave."

Segun's regretful tone burned Yomi's chest. His brother's separation from his wife of ten years had shocked the family. Particularly because Miriam, who'd been with Segun since secondary school in England, had cited infidelity as the reason for their major quarrel last year.

Although Yomi had tried not to pry, when he'd eventually confronted his brother about the accusation from Miriam, Segun had been vague and had all but admitted guilt.

He still couldn't believe Segun capable of infidelity. His devotion to his wife had been unparalleled. Exemplary. Besides, Segun had always been straight as an arrow. There had to be more to the story. But since Segun had refused to go into details, he'd never pressed further. He'd just assumed the separation would be temporary when tempers cooled off. Now, hearing about the possibility of divorce between them shook him to the core.

"How are Taiwo and Kehinde coping with this?"

"They're as fine as any nine-year-old could be about such things. I'm glad they're twins and have each other for support."

"I'm really sorry, Segun. And tell the girls their Uncle Yomi will visit soon and take them to the movies."

"They'll really like that. Anything to take their minds off their parents' failure at marriage."

"Okay, bro. Let me know when they would like to go."

Yomi stared at his brother sadly for moments. Segun looked completely different from him and Kunle. Although they were all slightly above six feet tall with a similar athletic build, Segun stood out amongst the three brothers because of his very dark mahogany complexion inherited from his late mother.

The fact that they were half-brothers had never made a difference to him or Kunle. Segun had pretty much been raised by their mother, having lost his own mother at the tender age of two from a ghastly road traffic accident.

They had all grown up together, their family bond strong. In fact, six years older than Kunle and eight years his senior, Segun had been the perfect big brother, protecting them from bullies. He'd constantly been the pride and joy of their father for his impeccable behaviour and excellent academic performance. This had sometimes made Yomi jealous when they were much younger.

However, as the years went by, he had begun to respect Segun a lot, seeking his advice for serious matters. He'd come to understand and appreciate his brothers for their different approaches to life. Segun was the thinker, who usually helped him out with complex emotional problems, and he could always count on Kunle whenever he wanted to have a good time and relax. Despite their differences, they loved one another, which was all that mattered.

"So, mate, forget about me and my bloody woes, and tell me about your love interest. What's her name?"

Segun's question brought his mind back to the present. He lifted his now lukewarm tea to his lips and sipped. "Emem Akpan."

"Oh, a Calabar *bird*. She already sounds interesting."

Yomi smiled. "Actually, she's from Akwa Ibom. And yes, she's fascinating."

"So, what's happened between you two? You're in love, but she doesn't feel you?" Segun queried, an eyebrow raised.

"Well, not exactly. I think she *does* feel me, but for some reason, she's fighting it."

"How so?"

Yomi relaxed in his seat and filled Segun in about Emem, how he'd met her, and about the four amazing weeks they'd spent together. Unwilling to divulge the information without her consent, he deliberately didn't reveal her identity as Sasha from the radio show. He ended by telling his brother about their argument five days ago.

"Man, an ultimatum? Why on Earth did you do that?" Segun asked when Yomi had finished speaking.

"I don't know," he replied, shrugging. "I just don't want to be her booty call. I love her too much to settle for that."

Segun didn't speak for moments as he nursed his cup of tea.

Yomi tried to guess his thoughts although he already suspected what they were. "You think I was too hasty, don't you?"

"Well, yes, Yomi. Sometimes, we've got to settle for what we have in our hands first, nourish it, savour it, before we go demanding more. What's that saying about a bird in a hand being better than a thousand in the bushes?"

His brother paused, and then looked at him squarely. "You love her. Stay with her, discover more about her, and give her a chance to feel the same way you do. If you get to be booty-called in the meantime, enjoy the hell out of that shit, too. Lord knows I'd give anything to have Miriam ring me up for a booty call."

Yomi's lips tugged into a small smile. He loved talking to Segun whenever he felt confused like this. His brother had a way of always bringing a different perspective and simplifying complicated issues.

"Thanks, bro. Makes a lot of sense."

"Cool, mate. Go get your woman. Don't make my mistakes. I should have grovelled to get my wife back, and now, she wants out."

Yomi eyed his brother with gratitude.

"Thanks again." He reached out and clasped his hand in his. "So don't give up. It's not over with Miriam. It can't be."

"Thanks, Yomi," Segun said, patting the back of his hand.

CHAPTER SIXTEEN

"What do you think about this one?" Natalie asked, swirling around in the ankle-length red dress that clung to her slender frame and highlighted her honey-brown complexion. She eyed her reflexion in the tall mirror anxiously as she did.

"It's not your style, Natalie," Emem muttered from her seat in the dressing room. Natalie had dragged her to *Silk and Style*, an upscale retailer on famed Banana Island. Its couture fashion wasn't really her thing. "And it's too expensive."

The cheapest dress here likely cost about half her monthly salary, and she couldn't fathom how people could afford shopping here on a daily basis. Or how Natalie could contemplate buying the dress she wore.

Of course, she knew that as a major investment banker in one of the most prestigious firms in Lagos, Natalie was very well paid. Plus, her generous and wealthy boyfriend, Chidi, owned several successful businesses, including a fleet of high-end hotels.

Still, the need for her friend to spend a hundred and twenty thousand Naira on an average-looking dress just because it was imported from Paris made her queasy.

"I know, Emem, but I'm visiting Chidi's hometown for the first time and meeting his very critical grandmother—the Queen of Sheba." Natalie rolled her eyes, and Emem chuckled. "I know they all think I'm a gold digger. So, I want to show them that I have my own money."

"What makes you think they won't assume that Chidi gave you the money and resent you anyway?" she asked wryly, shrugging. "Why go through all this?"

"You're right ..." Natalie paused. "It's just that ... All my life, I've rebelled against being this ... this person." She pointed to her reflection in the mirror.

"What person? I don't get it."

"This so-in-love-I'll-turn-myself-inside-out person. Just to impress his family."

Emem's eyes widened. She hadn't suspected the depth of her friend's feelings for Chidi. Natalie had always played down her relationship with him as a little more than casual. Although now, thinking about it, she remembered how much Natalie altered her schedule just to accommodate Chidi whenever he was in town. Something she rarely did for anyone else.

"I mean, I moved to Lagos five years ago full of steam to rise to the top of my firm," Natalie continued, unzipping the dress by the side. "And I did. On my own, without selling my soul. I wanted to rule the finance industry. Eventually become my own boss ..."

"You still can—"

"No, not anymore," Natalie interjected. "I'm in love with a multi-millionaire who worships the ground I walk on."

"I'm still trying to see the negative in this narrative, Natalie."

"Well, we can't both be going for business meetings if we get married and have a family. One of us has to take a step back, be the caregiver, the nurturer."

"That's absurd."

"Absurd, but true. It always happens. And it can't be Chidi. Many people depend on him for employment." Natalie slipped the dress down her body carefully. "My mother was the best resident general surgeon in Uni Port Teaching Hospital until she got pregnant with me.

Now, people younger than her are making discoveries while she is content being a regular surgeon."

"It doesn't have to happen that way. You can still rule the financial world."

"Not anymore, Emem. I'm pregnant ... forty-one years old and pregnant."

"What? I'm going to be an auntie?" She jumped out of her chair and pulled her friend into a warm embrace. "Congratulations, I'm so happy for you!"

"Thanks. I'm so excited, and Chidi is over the moon, too. He wants to get married straight away. Hence the planned trip to his hometown, so I can meet his ogre grandmother, the originator of their family dynasty. Her approval is paramount for a good marriage between us." She smiled as she spoke, rubbing her palm over her still flat belly.

"Oh, this is such good news!" Emem squealed. "We'll make your wedding a grand occasion ..."

"Great. I love Chidi—an Igbo man who loves his home town and is family-oriented," Natalie continued in a solemn voice. "But I'm scared of turning into one of those Igbo wives, you know ... the ones that go about spending their husband's money and nursing babies, the ones who are constantly in the village being hailed as *Oliaku*, or *Lolo*. I vowed never to be that person. Ever." She scrunched up her face in disgust.

"Trust me, although you are fully Igbo, Natalie Okoye, you'll never be that Igbo," Emem assured, her tone laced with amusement. "Besides, I'll kill you if you ever become that."

"Promise me, Emem. Promise me, please."

Natalie's desperate plea tickled Emem, and she had to swallow back the chuckle bubbling up in her throat.

"I promise."

They fell silent as she helped Natalie put the ugly dress back on the hanger.

"Natalie, congrats. Chidi's a good man. And he loves you. You'll not lose your individuality because of him. I'll keep reminding you of your own dreams no matter how many children you pop out."

"Thanks, Emem. That means a lot to me. Now, let's find another dress."

"Yes, and preferably one that's less drab and more affordable."

"Makes sense."

Emem waited about ten minutes outside the cloakroom for Natalie to change back into her jeans and T-shirt. They strolled out of the store, laughing hard at the daggers the saleswoman shot at them with her eyes for leaving without purchasing a blessed thing.

Hours later, having bought a much more attractive purple dress from *Mullan Designs*—a more understated boutique with reasonable prices—they were settled on the sofa in Emem's apartment, snacking on boiled groundnuts.

"So, it's truly over between you and Yomi, huh?" Natalie commented, cracking a shell of nuts with her teeth.

Emem froze. She'd really hoped to avoid talking about Yomi, because just the thought of him made her ache with sadness. She missed him like crazy. Six days of not seeing or hearing from him, and she couldn't stop thinking about him.

On many occasions throughout the week, she'd come close to walking over to his apartment unannounced and knocking on his door to beg for another chance, but had stopped herself each time. Not to mention the multiple text messages she'd typed and not sent, deleting them immediately instead. She knew that she couldn't give in. It was best this way. No point becoming more deeply involved in a relationship that was bound to fail.

"Yes," she answered simply, although her throat felt tight with the regret that sat heavily on her chest.

"I didn't quite understand your reason, though."

"I told you, he's moving too fast ..."

"And?"

"I don't want to give him the impression that there could be anything more between us."

Natalie sighed. "Emem, why are you being so hard on yourself? Why are you making things so complicated?"

"Because they are, Natalie!" she snapped, not meaning to raise her voice, but despair making her lash out at her friend. "You know as well as I do that he would eventually want children. Why put him through a relationship when I can't give him any?"

"Has he asked you to give him children?"

"No."

"Has he asked you to marry him?"

"No."

"So, the reason you're denying yourself a chance at happiness is because he asked you to meet his family?" Natalie's tone was incredulous, her forehead furrowed.

"It's not that simple. From meeting his family, it could lead to something more serious. I'm not willing to go so far with him only to crash-land because he can't accept my shortcomings."

"Have you told him about it?"

"No. And I don't want to."

She found it extremely hard thinking about it. She didn't want anyone else to know. Especially Yomi. She didn't want his pity if he left her, or his altruism if he stayed.

"What if you tell him and it doesn't change anything? What if he still wants you regardless?"

Natalie's question echoed in her brain, the possibility filling her with unreserved hope. Then, she remembered the look in Yomi's eyes when they'd sat beside a family at a restaurant two weeks ago. The dream that had reflected in their dark depths when he'd gazed back at her after staring at the beautiful baby close to them had been very revealing. He wanted a family. She could tell without a doubt. And she couldn't knowingly be with him when she couldn't give him one. That would be the ultimate act of selfishness. Better to cut her losses and leave before they got in too deep.

"I can't let him give up his dream of having a family because of me."

"There are other ways to have children, Emem."

"Says the pregnant woman!" she snapped, and immediately regretted her words. "I'm sorry, Natalie …"

Natalie waved a dismissive hand at her.

"I know you didn't mean it, Emem." She sucked in a deep breath and draped an arm around Emem's shoulders. "For once, don't think about the future, my dear. You were with Ejike for five years, moved to Lagos, and changed your life for him. Are you married to him?"

Knowing it was a rhetorical question, Emem didn't answer, and Natalie didn't wait for her to respond, either.

"No. So, why halt a good relationship because of the possibility of marriage? You could get sick of Yomi in two months, anyway, or vice versa, and this whole worry becomes moot. Might as well have a good time with a man who cares about you now. Enjoy the now, dear. We can't guarantee tomorrow."

"I just don't want to get hurt again," Emem whispered.

"And who says you will? Be good to yourself. Besides, how will you know if you don't try?" Natalie said, giving her an encouraging smile. "These are the wise words of a very clever person. You're an amazing psychologist, Emem. Heed your own advice."

She smiled back at her friend. "You're right, Natalie. Why am I overthinking things? A stunning man like Yomi likes me and wants me to meet his family. I feel the same way about him. What's so hard about going with the flow?"

"Exactly!" her friend affirmed. "There's nothing wrong with dating for the present. Deal with the future when the future happens."

Emem nodded, resolving to take a leap of faith and go with her heart instead of her head. Now, only one question remained to answer—was it too late to reach out to Yomi?

***

Peering through the window, Yomi watched as Emem embraced her friend Natalie by the opened gate of the compound. He poked his face through the small gap between the curtains, hoping to remain inconspicuous.

He'd adopted the same position earlier this afternoon when the hum of Emem's car engine driving into the apartment complex had grabbed his attention. Strange, but he could distinguish the sound of her Honda from the other vehicles belonging to occupants in the building.

After listening to her voice last night on the radio, he'd decided that he couldn't let her go. Even if he knew that for his self-preservation, he probably should. She had found a way under his skin like no other woman had, and he couldn't quite comprehend it. The only fact he was absolutely certain of was that he wouldn't give up without a fight.

So, this Saturday, he'd woken up, had an early morning run, returned for a quick shower, and driven off to purchase a bouquet of roses. But when he'd arrived home, he had found Emem's car absent. With his muscles tense and his entire body on full alert, he'd waited in his apartment like a caged animal for her return. She had come back mid-afternoon, but to his disappointment, with company.

His eyes focused on her as she waved at Natalie who waved back, stepping into a taxi. As Emem spun towards the building, her gaze jumped to his apartment window, and his heart crashed forcefully into his chest.

"Shit!" he cursed, ducking back behind the curtains. Had she seen him spying on her like a bloody stalker?

Yomi's heart drummed in his chest, and his stomach clenched, but that didn't prevent him from slowly sliding his face back towards the gap in the curtain.

She remained standing there, looking lovely in a floral summer dress, eyes locked in position at his window as though she could see him. Could she? Although he knew the thick beige drapes shielding his windows provided adequate cover, the intensity of her gaze made his confidence waver.

For seconds, she lingered, face drawn in concentration as she continued to peer at his window. Then, she began to move towards the entrance of the building, eyes fierce with determination.

Instinctively, he knew she was coming over to his apartment. He moved away from the window and rushed towards his front door, pulse skittering in helpless anticipation.

Blood pounded in his ears, drowning out any other sound but the heavy thumping of his heart. After an agonising week of not seeing Emem, touching her, she was coming over to his apartment. To yell? To tell him to fuck off and stop spying on her? He didn't know. It didn't matter what she wanted to say to him. Excitement surged through his veins at the prospect of seeing her beautiful face up close again, inhaling her lavender scent.

The light tap on the door knocked the breath out of his lungs, making him feel faint. He had to take quick breaths in succession to get his lungs working again. Damn! This woman had him by the balls.

"Who is it?" he asked, knowing his tone sounded phoney because of the tremor in his voice.

"Emem." A brief pause. "Can I come in?"

Yomi unlocked and opened the door, fingers shaking from a mixture of eagerness and nervousness.

They stood there, gazes locked for seconds. His gut twisted as he fought the desire to reach out and pull her into his apartment, lock the door, and throw the keys far away. He wanted to keep her in his life. Demand she stay—beg her to stay.

"I'm sorry, Yomi."

Her soft voice permeated his frenzied thoughts. His heart melted.

"Oh, Emem," he muttered, hauling her into his arms almost forcefully. "I missed you so bloody much."

"Yomi, I'm sorry. I missed you, too," she whimpered, holding him close, running her palms down his back, the touch of her hands heating his skin through his T-shirt.

Groaning, he lowered his head and captured her mouth with his, kicking the door shut as he moved her farther into the sitting room.

A low, throaty moan escaped her lips as she opened her mouth for the penetration of his tongue. With a greed that he couldn't control, he swept it inside her hot mouth, tasting, sucking, drinking from the sweetness within. He could never get enough of kissing Emem. She had the softest of lips, the most eager tongue. She gave as much as she took.

Her hands roamed under his shirt and gripped the skin of his back, the exquisite sensation of her palms against his bare flesh arousing him to an almost unbearable point. His penis hardened painfully, demanding escape from the confines of his shorts.

Feeling his control slipping away, he pulled back abruptly, breaking contact with her mouth. Her harsh sigh of frustration in his ears struck like a sword slicing through his restraint. But he held himself still. Although tempting, lifting and pinning Emem against the wall to ravish her mercilessly wasn't ideal at the moment. Not while they still had uncertainties between them. They needed to talk.

"Bloody hell, Emem," he rasped, pressing his forehead down on hers, taking deep breaths in and out as he struggled to bring his body under control. "You do something to me ..."

The heat from her laboured breaths as she clung to him seared his skin.

"Emem," he whispered, tilting her face towards him with his thumb. Her eyes fluttered open, and he could see the wetness of tears glistening in them. "I didn't mean to rush you," he murmured, trailing his thumb across her jaw in a slow caress.

"You didn't, Yomi ..." she protested.

He stopped her with a quick brush of his lips on hers. "Yes, I did. And I apologise."

"Don't. I want to go with you to meet your family." She paused, giving him a sweet, shy smile. "As your girlfriend."

Joy expanded his chest. His heart soared.

"You don't have to, Emem. I'll take things as slowly as you—"

She held a finger across his lips to silence him. "I want to." Moving that finger over his lower lip, she added in a hoarse voice, "I'm falling in love with you, Yomi Oladipo."

"Oh, Emem!" He drew her back into his arms, crushing her body with his in a heated embrace. "I love you!"

He pulled back and gazed into her twinkling eyes, his throat tight with the happiness that filled him.

"I love you. I love you," he chanted, planting multiple kisses all over her face.

She broke into a fit of giggles. The sound of her laughter, pleasant and melodious, was like music to his ears. A sound he hoped to hear for the rest of his life.

CHAPTER SEVENTEEN

The light pressure of Yomi's palm against the small of her back did nothing to calm the tension that billowed in Emem's belly as he assisted her from the passenger side of his shiny, black SUV.

They were finally at his family home after enduring an arduous fifty-five-minute drive because of heavy traffic. The time had arrived. Soon, she would be meeting the Oladipos. A major step in their budding relationship.

Even though she'd convinced herself that it didn't matter what anyone else thought about her and Yomi being together, there was a part of her that cared about his family's opinion.

Taking in a calming breath, she darted her gaze to Yomi. He looked handsome and relaxed in a dark brown T-shirt and a pair of black jeans. A thin gold chain—her birthday gift to him—hung around his neck.

With his long locks packed neatly away from his face, she appreciated the stunning angles of his chiselled cheekbones under luminous eyes draped with thick lashes. A shadow of stubble surrounded his jaw and mouth, drawing attention to luscious, full lips.

"Are you okay?" he asked, stretching those lips into a charming smile that gave her a glimpse of perfect dimples.

"Yes," she answered, smiling back. "Just a little nervous."

"Don't be. You look amazing."

Her smile widened. She knew she did. Having spent the day before trying on countless outfits for this occasion, with Natalie fussing over her non-stop, Emem was glad she'd settled for this red, knee-length, sleeveless dress, and the four-inch black pumps on her feet. Yomi's reaction when he'd picked her up at the apartment had been all the approval she'd needed.

"Thanks," she said, clasping his outstretched hand and following him down the granite pathway leading towards the front door.

As they strolled together, she swept her gaze around the marble-walled house. Although he had told her earlier that it was an eight-bedroom home, the massive size gave the impression of a hotel containing more rooms. The building curved into a semicircle at the edge of an extensive compound.

"Wow, Yomi, this house is gorgeous!" she gushed, unable to curtail the awe she felt.

He grinned. "Thanks. But it's my father's home. Believe me, I lived a very modest life in London and hardly ever stayed here, except for a few half-terms and summer holidays."

"Still, look at the size of this compound. And the huge house ..."

"Yes, well, that's the architect in him. He wanted his own home to be an advertisement for the firm."

"Well, I'm sure it works. The place is very impressive."

"Yes, it is," he said, nodding in agreement.

She suddenly halted just as they reached the front door, her pulse rate speeding up as panic began to set in. Perspiration started prickling the skin under both arms.

"I don't want to ruin your birthday, b-but I'm worried. Wh-what if your family hates me?" she sputtered.

"Oh, come on! What's not to like?" His dark gaze swept over her. "You're gorgeous, intelligent, and I love you, so they'll all love you. In fact, I'm worried my brother, Kunle, will love you way too much and make a move on you."

She chuckled. "Oh, Yomi, I love you, too. But I'm serious ... Won't they think I'm a cougar trying to wreck your life?"

Yomi bellowed with laughter, the firm chords of his neck contracting as he did. Unexpectedly, he whirled her towards him and drew her into his arms, lowering his mouth to hers for a searing wet kiss.

"Wreck my life, baby. Wreck it in every possible way," he muttered in a low, hoarse voice when he lifted his head.

"Oh, Yomi, my lipstick ..." she protested laughingly, wiping the bright red hue off his lips with her thumb. "Now, it's all over you. I hope some is still on me. I may have to reapply—"

The door swung open, interrupting her.

"Yomi, you fool! Don't attack this poor woman by the front door," a tall, light-skinned man quipped in a gregarious tone.

They turned simultaneously towards the intruder. Yomi broke into a grin as he pulled him into a bear hug.

"Kunle, my man!" he greeted cheerily.

"Happy thirtieth, Yomi, bro! Welcome to the club."

Yomi's brother looked a lot like him, even down to sharing similar striking dimples. Although slightly slimmer and with a low cropped haircut, Kunle could pass for Yomi's twin brother.

As Kunle withdrew from Yomi's embrace, he eyed her quizzically.

"You must be the lovely Emem," he said, a knowing grin splitting his face. "I've heard so much about you."

Her cheeks warmed. What on Earth had Yomi been telling his family about her?

"Yes, she is. Kunle, meet Emem, my woman," Yomi said, draping his arm round her waist. "Emem, my brother, Kunle."

"Nice to meet you, Kunle," she said shyly, offering her hand in greeting.

"Likewise. Welcome, dear," Kunle said, a wolfish smile playing on his lips. He took her hand in his and planted a soft kiss on her knuckles. "You're even lovelier than I imagined," he said, his tone sounding a lot huskier than it had earlier.

"Okay, now, hands off, bro," Yomi muttered, snatching her hand away from his brother's hold as he glared at him. "Such a bloody flirt. You can't help yourself."

"Calm down, Yomi. Just being friendly," Kunle said, chuckling. He turned to her. "Oh, my brother must like you a lot," he added, giving her a conspiratorial wink. "Never seen him this jealous."

Emem winked back but said nothing, totally enjoying the easy banter between the brothers and also secretly thrilled to hear this information from Kunle.

"Shut up. Let's go in before I bust your head," Yomi snorted, holding onto her hand and leading her inside. "But Kunle is right," he whispered in her ear as they strolled into the house. "You are lovelier than seems possible."

Fingers entwined with his, she followed them through a long hallway that led to a spacious sitting room.

"Have a seat, babe," Yomi said, offering her the closest sofa to where she stood. "Want anything to drink?"

She shook her head and sank into the plush leather. "Not right now."

She swept her gaze around in appreciation of the stylishly decorated room adorned with dark leather furnishing that faced a massive flat screen television anchored to the wall. Antique-looking glass ornaments situated at various corners of the room gave the place an aristocratic ambience.

"Nice place," she murmured.

Emem focused her attention on the large family photograph on the wall. In it, Yomi stood smiling in the middle of his two brothers, surrounding their father, who sat in a thrown-like chair. All dressed in impeccable white *agbada*, they looked regal—like Yoruba royalty.

She already knew that Yomi's parents had divorced a long time ago, and that his mother had been unfaithful to his father, but the fact that she wasn't in the picture saddened her. It would have been a perfect family portrait with her sitting there with them.

"Where's everyone?" Yomi asked, interrupting her musings. "It's almost two p.m."

He strolled over and settled on the armrest beside her and caressed her shoulder lightly.

"You know our people. Keeping to *Nigerian time*," Kunle answered. "Dad's just getting dressed, and Segun rang to tell us he's on his way."

"Bringing the twins?" Yomi queried, a hopeful lilt in his voice.

"No. They're with Miriam today, performing at a community children's choir event. Segun just left the venue a few minutes ago."

"Oh, too bad. I was really hoping to see them." He turned to her. "My nieces. The ones I told you about. Amazing, clever girls. I'll take you to meet them soon."

Her chest constricted. The pride in his eyes as he spoke filled her with guilt. Yomi obviously adored his nieces and would clearly be the same way with his own children. How could she deprive him of the chance to be a father? Would that be fair to him?

She knew that she needed to have an honest talk with him about that soon. But when? For the week they'd been back together, they'd been having such a wonderful time that she hadn't wanted to ruin it with reality. Plus, with every passing day, it was becoming increasingly difficult to bring up the issue. How did one even start that conversation?

"You okay?" Yomi's concerned question pulled her out of her troubled thoughts. "You zoned out on us for a minute."

"Oh, yes, I'm fine," she lied, turning her face away from him quickly to hide from his intense perusal. She willed herself to smile when she lifted her gaze back to him. "I was just admiring the lovely pic—"

"Happy birthday, son!"

A loud baritone voice boomed from the entrance to the sitting room. They all whipped their gazes in unison to find Chief Oladipo by the door.

Relief rushed through Emem as she rose to her feet. *Saved by the bell.*

"Good afternoon, sir."

Yomi and his brother echoed the greeting, both rising abruptly and then falling onto the shiny white terrazzo floor in prostration to him as though in prayer.

Although Emem knew this to be a customary acknowledgment of elders in the Yoruba culture, she'd never actually witnessed it up close. The almost automatic show of respect was so appealing that it made her feel compelled to join the ritual. However, she bent her knees halfway to the ground as she'd seen done multiple times by women in Lagos. "Good afternoon, sir."

"Good afternoon, everyone," Chief Oladipo replied, motioning for his sons to rise with a wave of his hand. He moved farther into the room, took her hand in his for a firm handshake. "You must be the lovely Emem Akpan. It's finally nice to meet the woman who's put a constant smile on my son's face these past few weeks."

"Oh, yes, thank you, sir. Nice to meet you, too," Emem returned, bursting with the joy flooding her senses at the heart-warming reception from Yomi's father.

"You are welcome to our home as we celebrate Yomi's special day as a family. Come on, let's head over to the dining room. My fantastic chef prepared an enormous feast for this occasion." He smoothed his palm over the front of his kaftan top as he spoke, the deep ebony hue of his skin contrasting dramatically with the shiny white material.

"Thank you, sir," she said, smiling up at Yomi's father.

Tall like his sons, Chief Oladipo had an imposing presence because of his heavyset stature. He wasn't particularly overweight, but the expanse of his wide shoulders made him seem bigger than he actually was.

Still beaming with happiness, she linked arms with Yomi as Chief Oladipo led them all to the next room.

"Wow, this is huge," she gushed, gaze darting around the long mahogany table covered with a vast array of dishes fit for a royal feast.

The aroma of warm food saturated her nostrils, making her almost dizzy with hunger. Her stomach growled loudly in response, and they all laughed.

"Don't worry, it's allowed. I'm famished, too," Yomi murmured, planting a soft kiss on her forehead to stave off her embarrassment.

Kunle patted her back in support. "Don't mind my father, Emem. He never does anything small. Everything has to be done in excess with him. Whenever he invites any of us for dinner, we don't eat two days beforehand, just to prepare. You'll soon hear my own stomach rumble."

"Don't blame me for your stomach problems, Kunle. We all know you're lactose intolerant," Chief Oladipo teased, and loud laughter reverberated in the room.

"But what about Segun?" Yomi asked when everyone quietened again. He glanced at his watch. "Shouldn't we wait for him?"

"I'm here now. And guess who I bumped into at the gate when I arrived?" announced a deep voice sounding eerily similar to Chief Oladipo's.

As Emem spun towards Segun, she noticed the colour drain from Yomi's face seconds before she spotted the other new arrival to the party. A petite woman with tanned olive skin, long blond hair, and delicate facial features, her blue eyes sparkling with hope as she stood by the door.

Undeniably, a face that could not be mistaken because of the strong resemblance she bore to her son. Yomi's mother.

CHAPTER EIGHTEEN

Harsh whooshing sounds echoed in Yomi's ears as he remained stock still staring at his mother. Of all the things he had expected today, seeing her hadn't been one of them.

Seven bloody years, he'd managed to avoid being in the same room with her. Had celebrated six birthdays in her absence. Everyone in the family knew to ensure he was informed whenever she was present, so that he avoided the location until she had left.

They'd initially tried to bridge the gap between mother and son, setting up mediating phone calls and meetings between them, and in the early years, he'd attempted to understand, had even managed to endure her presence without losing it. Until she'd attended a family event with her toy-boy hanging onto her arm and openly flaunting their relationship without any sensitivity.

Absolutely disgusted by her behaviour that evening, he'd detached himself completely from her, unwilling to set his eyes on her again. Despite the entreaties from his family, he hadn't budged. The last attempt organised by Kunle to put them in the same room had ended in an embarrassing word match in which he had used a derogatory word to describe his mother. One that he had never used on any other woman.

He had immediately regretted it, but had also been annoyed that he'd been put in that situation in the first place—forced against his will to see a woman he considered dead to him.

How dare she come here now? How *dare* she? Knowing today was his birthday. Bad enough that he'd discovered her debauchery on his birthday. A day which had been forever tainted with the image of his mother acting like a whore. He'd worked hard to dissociate that negative emotion from his day of celebration. Mostly by avoiding her like she had an infectious disease.

Prolonged awkwardness filled the air as everyone remained silent, the room seemingly frozen in time. Then, he heard his father's voice, the deep rumble shattering the inertness in the atmosphere.

"Amanda, welcome," Chief Oladipo said, moving over to embrace his ex-wife and kissing her on both cheeks. "You look ever so lovely."

"Thanks, Dele, and so do you," she responded, stroking his arm gently. "Have you been working out?"

The low chuckle from his father grated like tiny daggers on Yomi's nerves.

"Yes, as a matter of fact, I have," Chief Oladipo murmured. "At least one person has noticed."

His amorous tone irritated Yomi even more. The utter weakness the chief had for his cheating ex-wife annoyed him. How could he be so accepting of her? Especially when she had abandoned him—the family— to marry a man half her age. How?

"Mum!" Kunle rushed over and lifted Amanda in his arms, twirling her around. "Nice to see you!"

"Put me down, lad. I'm too old for this," she squealed, pressing a kiss on Kunle's forehead, clearly delighted to see him.

Cheering filled the room as Kunle lowered her to the ground, Yomi's father and two brothers beaming with joy. The entire family appeared happy to receive her. As always. Everyone but him.

Suddenly remembering Emem's presence in the room, he turned to her. She also stood motionless, her gaze trained on him, forehead furrowed in concern—an instinctive stance of solidarity with him that he found totally mind-blowing. She hadn't made any move to welcome his mother because he hadn't. If there had been any iota of doubt about his love for her, this moment had erased it completely.

He relaxed his posture and held out a hand to her.

"Let's get the hell out of here," he murmured, needing to escape the room and hold onto her, draw some comfort from her sweet softness.

"Yomi, my son ..."

Amanda's voice crashed through his thoughts, making him break contact with Emem's eyes, the only solace he'd found since his mother's unexpected arrival had shattered his jubilant mood.

"I am *not* your son!" he growled through clenched teeth, the simmering anger boiling in him suddenly let loose.

"It's been over ten years, Yomi! Why can't we put the past behind us?"

"You'd like that, wouldn't you?" he retorted. "A complete absolution for your disgraceful act ... well, I will not forgive you for being a liar and a cheat."

Her shocked gasp resounded in the room. Along with Chief Oladipo's deep, cautionary grunt.

"Yomi," Chief Oladipo warned, but Amanda raised a hand to stop him.

"No, let him say what he wants to say, Dele. Let him get it all off his chest. Maybe we can all move forward afterwards."

"Oh, you really want to hear what I have to say, do you?" Yomi ground out. "It was on my bloody birthday. I was the one who saw you with that boy ... on my birthday!"

153

"That boy ... that man is now my husband, Yomi! I was wrong, I know I was, but I've apologised many times."

He barked out a harsh laugh. "Saying sorry for leaving your family. Oh, that's rich. You think a simple sorry can erase what you did to us? To me?"

"To you? I didn't do anything to you, Yomi. I cheated on my husband ... *my husband*. Not you. I didn't abandon you, either. *You* left— just up and moved into a flat. I remember trying very hard to get you to move back home. But I couldn't stop you. You were eighteen. An adult. You wanted nothing to do with me."

"And I still don't. Why won't you leave me the hell alone? Why?"

"Because you are my son. I love you. I want to be in your life."

"Stop calling me your son."

"You may not want to hear it, but that's what you are. My son. And I'm begging for your forgiveness. I want you to forgive me." Her voice broke off. "Everyone else seems to have done so ... to understand ..."

"Well, I refuse to understand how you could do that to a man who loved you, who worked hard to provide for his family ... and for what? For a young boy!"

"Your father and I had problems way before. You're old enough to understand that nothing is that simple."

"Yes, it is," he spat out, his tone raw with anger. "You're an ungrateful cheat, and I want nothing to do with you. Not now. Not ever. It's as simple as can be."

A sob broke out from her—a heart-wrenching sound that pulled at his heart strings. God, why had she come today of all days? He had only wanted to celebrate this happy day with his family. Now, here he was, dealing with emotions he had long buried.

The truth was that his mother had shattered all his illusions of the protected life he'd created in his mind for himself. As a mixed-race teenager living in London, he'd felt confused many times, had struggled with his identity. But his parents' love for each other had made him feel secure. Had solidified his bi-racial heritage—half English and half Nigerian. As long as they'd been together, he'd been able to cope with both sides of his identity.

But that very day when he'd discovered his mother's infidelity, all that he'd thought he understood about himself had come crashing down. With that muddled emotion, self-doubt had also arisen.

His parents' divorce had been hard on him, particularly because of his father's definitive relocation to Nigeria afterward. A country he had visited just a few times with him during summer holidays. He'd felt a part of his identity—his Nigerian heritage threatened by that, that he'd lose it in the process. Gone. Disappeared. All because of his mother.

Yomi ground his jaw, the muscles of his face tight with the need to lash out more, but he dragged in a breath and turned back to Emem. He stretched his lips into a strained smile and reclaimed her hand. "Come on. Let's go."

She made a move to follow his lead, but Chief Oladipo stepped directly in front of them.

"Yomi." His tone sounded gentle as he grabbed Yomi's arm to stop him. "It's your birthday, and Emem's our guest. You can't let her leave like this."

"You should have thought about that when you invited this slut who calls herself a mother for my birthday celebration."

155

Before Yomi could take another step forward, Chief Oladipo lifted him by the collar and slammed his back against the nearest wall.

"You will never say that word to, or about, your mother, ever again, Yomi Oladipo. Is that clear?" he barked, his eyes bulging, and a vein at his temple pulsating.

"I don't get how you can defend her, Dad! I don't get it …"

"Is that clear?" his father snarled again, scrunching up the collar of his shirt together even tighter.

Yomi glared at his father, chest heaving and breath coming out in harsh grunts, annoyance and frustration billowing in his belly. He wanted to tell him to go to Hell, tell all of them to go to Hell, and storm out of this house. However, he dragged in a slow, calming breath and shifted his eyes to Emem.

She was standing beside Chief Oladipo, a palm resting over her abdomen in a self-protective gesture, as though trying to calm her own tension. Their gazes held for moments. Yomi sucked air into his lungs at the wariness registered in her eyes. There was also a softness in their dark depths, a flicker of understanding, yet a plea for peace.

All the tension within him seeped away immediately, the silent entreaty from Emem getting to him. He turned back to his father and nodded. "Okay, Dad."

"Listen, Yomi," Chief Oladipo said, releasing him and smoothing a palm over his crumpled shirt. "It's been many years. Forgive. And let's all try and move on."

His father's comment produced a storm of conflicting emotions that slammed into his chest. Why was it so easy for everyone else to do that but him? Why couldn't he just let go?

He swallowed past the lump that suddenly wedged his throat. "It's my birthday. And I want to have a good time. It's either she leaves, or I do. But we can't both be here. Not today. This is not the day to talk about all this."

"Yomi." It was Segun, this time. "Why don't we all just sit down and eat—"

"No, Yomi's right," Amanda said, her tone heavy with resignation. "I shouldn't have come here today. I'm sorry, Yomi." She reached into her purse, pulled out a gift-wrapped package, and lowered it onto the dining table. "Happy birthday, son," she murmured, a broken smile on her lips. "I'll leave now. But we do need to talk, Yomi. I'm staying at *Selfridge Hotel*, Ikeja. I'll be there 'til the end of the month. Your father knows my room number."

She turned to Chief Oladipo, and her smile widened.

"Thanks for trying," she whispered, strolling over to him and planting a soft kiss on his cheek. She swept her gaze around. "It was nice to see everyone today."

Finally, her eyes rested on Emem.

"Sorry about all of this. I hope to see you again under better circumstances," Amanda said, giving her a friendly smile.

Emem smiled back and nodded but said nothing. Yomi's gut clenched. He hated that she'd witnessed such ugliness the first time meeting his family. He wished he'd controlled himself better. It was just that he had not anticipated his mother's presence. Maybe if he had, he'd have managed to restrain himself. Okay, who was he kidding? He wouldn't have come at all if he'd had any inkling that she would show up.

Still, he wished his family hadn't blindsided him, leaving him vulnerable, raw. And all in front of Emem. What did she think about him now? Had his family drama scared her off?

As though sensing his uncertainty, she walked over to him and draped her arms around his midriff. A show of support that dissipated his worries immediately, making him want to ignore everyone else in the room, pull her to him, and crush her into a tight embrace.

"See you all later," Amanda said, turning to leave. The atmosphere remained tense as she strolled out, her shoulders slumped.

A sudden sadness filled Yomi, constricting his chest. He wanted to call her back, tell her they could work things out, but he pushed back the instinct, his voice swallowed up by his muddled feelings towards his mother.

Moments of strained silence followed her departure.

"Okay, everyone. Let's eat. The food is getting cold," Kunle said finally, breaking the silence.

"I agree." Chief Oladipo moved over to the table and plonked himself on a chair. He swept his gaze to Yomi and Emem. "Come and sit. Let's try and enjoy the rest of today's celebration."

Yomi nodded. He held onto Emem and guided her to the table. Planting a soft kiss on her forehead as she took the seat that he'd pulled out for her, he resolved to do exactly that—enjoy his birthday celebration. He would deal with his mother on another day.

The atmosphere seemed to lighten again as Kunle and Segun joined them at the table.

***

"I can't eat any more!" Kunle groaned, patting his tummy. "My stomach will explode if I put another morsel into my mouth."

"You ate Chef Biola's special almond cake. Your stomach will soon explode regardless," Segun teased.

"I'm lactose-intolerant. Not severely diseased," Kunle protested, flashing a reproachful glare at his brother.

"That's not what the smell of the house suggests after every dinner party," Yomi snickered. "Let's just say the air freshener takes the bulk of the abuse."

"Go to Hell, assholes!" Kunle grunted, throwing his hands upwards in helpless surrender, an affronted expression on his face. They all rippled with laughter at his expense.

"Guys, guys, we have a guest," Chief Oladipo chided, although still shaking from his own laughter. "This is not appropriate dining table talk."

Emem waved a dismissive hand.

"Please, ignore me, I'm totally enjoying all of this," she said, raising her wine goblet to her lips, extremely amused.

Despite the awkward start to the dinner party, she was having a good time. She loved the relationship between Yomi and his brothers. They were jovial, fun together, and evidently loved each other. In contrast to her relationship with her siblings and parents. Growing up, her own family dinners had usually been solemn events with little or no conversation.

As she swept her gaze around the table, taking in the easy rapport in the family, she realised that all her anxiety about meeting Yomi's family had been unwarranted. They'd welcomed her with open arms, not asking too many personal questions. She'd felt free to talk about herself, and even for the first time ever, revealed she was Sasha from the radio show to new acquaintances.

"Well, we are glad you are, and that you came," Chief Oladipo said, cutting through her musings.

"I'm glad I did, too."

She smiled at Yomi's father. A burst of happiness erupted in her chest as he grinned back at her. She'd been worried about today for nothing.

CHAPTER NINETEEN

Hours later, Emem pushed open the door to Yomi's apartment. They'd arrived back home only about ten minutes ago. Having both decided to spend the night together at his place, she'd rushed over to her flat to change to more comfortable denim shorts and a blue tank top.

She locked the door with the spare key he'd given her and strolled over to the kitchen where she found him peering into the fridge.

"What? Are you still hungry after all we ate at your father's house?" she asked with incredulity.

He closed the fridge holding a mango, his eyes brimming with amusement. "A bit. Just searching for something to snack on."

"*Na wa o.* You are so lucky you can eat anything and remain slim. See me ..." She patted the slight bulge of her stomach. "Just one day of cheat-eating, and I'm a balloon."

Yomi grinned and reached out to caress her stomach. "And what a sexy balloon you are."

"Stop with the flattery. I'm going on a diet from tomorrow."

He rinsed the mango by the kitchen sink, then sank his teeth into it.

"Not flattery, babe. Facts." He held out the succulent fruit to her lips. "Want some?"

"Satan, get thee behind me," she grumbled, shaking her head even as she took a small bite. "I know your plan. To get me so fat that nobody else would want me."

161

"I hope it works." A roguish grin spread across his lips. "Because I swear, I couldn't stand the way Kunle's eyes were glued to you all day. I wanted to smash his face in."

She laughed out. "Trust me, I'm not his type. I'm not a famous, surgeon-carved celebrity."

A loud rumble of laughter erupted from him, causing his body to quake and the mango to slip from his fingers. Still trembling from the giggles that overtook him, he picked it off the floor and tossed it into the bin nearby.

Emem found herself chuckling, too, his profound amusement infecting her. "But it's true *nau*. Kunle's current girlfriend looks so artificial—fake boobs and an even faker ass."

"I know, babe. He seems drawn to those synthetic bimbos. We keep teasing him about it," Yomi said, wiping tears from his eyes with the back of his hand. He walked over to the kitchen sink, turned on the tap, and washed his hands. A sudden serious expression crossed his face when he whirled back to her. "Thanks for coming today. It wouldn't have been the same without you."

Her heart soared. His candour thrilled her immeasurably. "Thanks for inviting me, Yomi. I had a marvellous time."

Eyes blazing with purpose, he moved away from the sink and strolled towards her, stopping right in front of her. Brushing a thumb over her cheek, he whispered, "You were amazing today. Everyone in the family told me that you're the real deal, that I should never let you go. But I already know that."

"Oh, Yomi ... thank you. And I loved meeting all of them," she said. "Your father is hilarious. And so is Kunle. Even reserved Segun has his moments."

"Ha! Don't let Segun's prim and proper act fool you. He can be a real hoot sometimes. He's the only one in the family who smokes weed. And very boldly in public."

She gasped. "What? I can't believe it! Segun and weed? He seems so ..."

Yomi chuckled.

"I know. Back in London, he and my mum would sit at the—"

He broke off, his jaw muscles contracting, the mention of his mother most likely triggering a negative emotion.

Emem fought back a sigh. Yomi obviously had *mummy issues*. While observing the heated exchange between his mother and him earlier, she had wondered if that was the reason why he wanted to be with her. Whether he saw her as a substitute mother.

But she'd pushed that worry away immediately. She wasn't that much older than him. Not even close. And she'd not noticed that in his dating habits. In fact, he'd admitted to her that she was the first older woman he'd ever dated.

"Yomi," she began softly, stroking his arm. "About your mother ..."

"I don't want to talk about her." A gruff declaration.

She let out a short sigh. "You both need to talk at some point. You can't keep avoiding her."

"And how many times do you talk to your own family, Emem, huh?"

Her jaw dropped, a shocked gasp emitting through her parted lips.

"Uncalled for!" she snapped, spinning away from him in annoyance.

The firm grasp of his hand on her arm stopped her as he whirled her back to him.

"I'm sorry, Emem," he murmured, draping his arms around her and crushing her in a tight embrace. "It's just that I hate talking about her. It takes me back to a very dark time of my life."

Holding him close, she cradled him against her.

"I understand," she whispered, stroking his back. "I understand."

"Please don't go, Emem. I need you. I need you."

"I'm here. Right here. I'm not going anywhere."

They stayed locked in each other's arms for a long moment, absorbing each other's essence. He lifted her, carrying her astride him, and set her on the kitchen counter.

"You're the light in my darkness, Emem," he muttered, kissing her softly on the mouth. "From the first time I heard your voice on the radio ..."

He trailed his tongue over the angle of her lips before capturing them with his.

Fervently, they kissed, bodies entwined, impatient fingers touching and gripping flesh and muscle.

"You're just perfect for me," he rasped.

His deep voice rang in her ears, setting her blood on fire.

"Oh, Yomi," she whimpered as she flung her arms around his neck, drawing him even closer to her as their mouths fused.

The atmosphere between them sizzled, changing from ire to sensual heat within seconds. As always, the passion between them proved all-consuming.

Emem dragged her hands over Yomi's back, grasped the edge of his shirt, and pulled it over his head, breaking contact with his mouth.

Not missing a beat, his lips descended on hers again, swirling his tongue inside the dark recesses, tangling with hers in a sweet, fiery rhythm.

Moist pleasure seeped from her core, making her throb with the need for him. She spread her legs wider, rotating her hips against the thick bulge in his sweatpants.

"Emem!"

A raw growl tore from his throat as his large hands cupped her bottom through her shorts. He squeezed the soft mounds of flesh and brought her heated centre flush against his hardness.

"You drive me crazy," he moaned, his mouth hot and wet against hers. "Whenever I'm with you ... pure joy ..."

His words excited her as much as the erotic sensation of his lips as he moved his head lower, scattering kisses and trailing his tongue over the sensitive skin of her neck.

Wanting more of his mouth action on her bare flesh, she pushed him back, reached for the edge of her tank top, and lifted it over her head.

"Aah ..." he groaned, eyes feasting on her lace-covered breasts.

He leaned forward to kiss her cleavage, but she shoved him away again, unfastening the front claps of her bra.

"Perfection!" he gasped, undisguised desire in his eyes.

He cupped a full breast in his hand. With reverent slowness, he lowered his head and fastened his mouth on a taut nipple.

Soft moans tumbled from her and ricocheted off the kitchen walls as Yomi made love to her breasts, skilfully treating each to the sweet torture of his hungry mouth.

Emem's body quivered with need, the nub between her thighs throbbing for release.

"Yomi ..." she whimpered, reaching between them to touch his erection.

Hard and long, it strained in her palm. She moved her hand, stroking up and down, her thumb brushing over the swollen tip.

A deep grunt erupted from him.

"You're killing me," he growled in a strained voice.

"Kill me, too, Yomi ... take me now."

Her demand seemed to destroy all his control. He pulled back from her abruptly. Almost roughly, he clutched the top of her shorts and dragged them down her thighs and legs.

"Damn!" he rasped. "No panties."

"What's the point?" She spread her legs in offering to him. "Happy birthday, baby."

"Lord!"

Eyes darkened with lust, he shoved his sweatpants down and held onto her hips, securing her at the edge of the kitchen counter.

"Guide me in," he muttered, teeth clenched tightly with need. "Lead me home."

Emem gazed into his eyes as she curled her fingers around his hard shaft and directed him to the entrance of her womanhood.

"Come in, Yomi," she whispered, parting her thighs wider in encouragement.

A relieved sigh gushed from deep within her when he thrust into her decisively, filling her, touching every nerve of her inner walls.

"You're my woman," he ground out, baring his teeth and grazing her jaw line. "Just made for me ... only me."

"Yes ...yes ..." she moaned, savouring the exquisite sensation of his thickness moving powerfully inside her. "Feels so good, Daddy. Don't stop ... don't stop ..."

His accurate thrusts repeatedly hit her at just the right spot, propelling her with a rapid pace towards the edge. He withdrew completely outside her and drove into her again, circling his hips as he did.

"Oh, God!" she cried out at the sheer pleasure that shot through her entire being from that skilful move. The angle of penetration was so precise that it pushed her over. "I'm coming ... oh, Yomi ... oh ..."

A shrill cry of fulfilment sprang from her throat as strong waves of ecstasy rocked her body in a powerful release.

Seconds later, he clutched her butt cheeks tightly, a guttural shout escaping his lips as he shuddered his climax.

"Emem."

His helpless whisper against her neck when he slumped onto her caused another spasm to tighten her core.

She let out a long sigh of satisfaction, squeezing her thighs around his narrow waist, and basking in the aftershocks of pleasure from his superb loving.

CHAPTER TWENTY

Breathing heavily, they clung to each other as their passions slowly ebbed. He, in a state of disarray with his pants bunched awkwardly around his ankles. Her, completely naked and legs spread apart on the kitchen counter.

Yomi tried to catch his breath. Emem had a way of making him lose control. This hadn't been the plan at all. On his bed lay scattered rose petals. He'd also run a warm bath with scented candles arranged at the corners of the bathroom.

They were supposed to have made love slowly after a nice soak, a sweet culmination to a wonderful birthday celebration.

Yet, here he was, nearly naked and clutching her in the kitchen after a mind-blowing quickie. He sighed inwardly. He really ought to control himself better. A sudden thought came to him, and he leaned away from her slightly.

"I didn't use a condom," he murmured, trailing a thumb over her jaw. "I'm sorry …"

"It's fine …" she said, giving him a sheepish smile. "Takes two to tango. I'm sorry, too."

He cradled her face in his hands. "I'm clean. Tested for STDs two months ago. I can retest if you want …"

"We'll both go. I'm clean, too. At least, when I last tested."

Moments of silence ensued. The cool air danced on his naked butt, but he was in no hurry to get dressed, enjoying just being near her, inhaling the smell of sex in the air between them.

"I won't mind, you know."

"Won't mind what?"

"If we just made a baby."

Her eyes widened, and her mouth popped open.

"I ... eh ..." she trailed off.

He planted a soft kiss on her mouth, gazing intently at her. An almost uncontrollable desire to blurt out that he wanted to marry her surged to his lips, but he held his tongue, swallowing the words he knew would most definitely scare her away. Instead, he kissed her again.

"I think about such things, you know, since I met you ... having a family with you ... a beautiful girl that looks just like you and has my sense of style." He gave her a playful wink, then grinned. "I know you'd be an amazing mother."

Her body became rigid, and her posture tensed. She placed both palms on his chest, pushing him away from her gently.

"Hey," he protested, pulling his pants back over his hips. "What's going on?"

"Nothing. I just ... please don't be too forward. I told you I wanted to take things slowly."

"I ... Emem, I didn't mean to rush you. I'm only saying if tonight results in a baby, I'd be delighted."

"Well, it won't," she snapped, jumping down the kitchen counter.

"It could happen, and I'd be thrilled if it—"

"We've been dating for only seven weeks, Yomi! Talking about making babies is too damn soon."

He started at her angry tone, confused. He hadn't meant to annoy or rush her. Hell, that was the last thing he had in mind. He didn't even know why she stood staring at him with daggers in her eyes. But in his state of confusion, he also saw something else apart from exasperation registered in their dark depths. Fear? Anxiety?

He sucked air into his lungs slowly, willing himself to relax. She was right. He shouldn't be rushing things. If she wasn't ready to commit to him yet, he'd wait until she was. And talking about babies seven weeks into their relationship seemed too intense.

"Let's not fight about this, okay?" He lifted her warm, naked body in his arms, wanting to erase the negative energy his remark had created. "What I'm trying to say, rather poorly, is that I'm in for the long haul no matter what. I love you."

Her body sagged as she melted into him. "I love you, too, Yomi. Let's just keep taking one day at a time."

He kissed the top of her head and nodded. Although he already knew exactly what he wanted, he also knew that seven weeks in a relationship would be considered too hasty by most people for making lasting plans.

If Emem wanted to take her time, he'd have to accept it, slow down until she came to grips with her feelings. And if they *had* made a baby tonight, he was confident that they'd make the best decision together.

***

Turning to her side on the bed, Emem stared at Yomi's sleeping form beside her. With his face relaxed, he looked so young and peaceful. He had the bed covers up to his shoulders, but he still curled up as though trying to ward off the cold.

She shifted her gaze to the air conditioner attached to the wall directly above them and smiled. Yomi always insisted on having it on and at the lowest temperature, even if he had to suffer through a chilly night.

According to him, the cool air kept mosquitoes away. "Those little blood suckers can't stand the cold like I can," he'd say. And she'd laugh every time, telling him that to her, malaria was a much more preferable illness to have than pneumonia.

He shivered in his sleep, pulling the bed cover higher over his jaw. Her attention refocused on his closed eyes. The long, curled lashes caressing his cheeks lent an almost effeminate quality to his facial features. Yet, no mistaking his masculinity when his dark eyes opened, the virility of his intense gaze.

Emem smiled. She'd never watched any man sleep, never felt the need to, but she'd awoken many times in the past week, staring at Yomi while he remained oblivious to her scrutiny, thinking about how right it felt lying beside him. A warm feeling tightened her chest as she watched him snooze. She loved him so very much. Without a doubt, she wanted a future with him.

Heaviness sat in her chest when she recalled the conversation they'd had in the kitchen. A baby. She'd give anything to be pregnant with his baby now. But that was impossible. It broke her heart that this man who she loved, who she'd do anything for, wouldn't experience what she now knew to be a desire of his—having a baby with her.

Why hadn't she told him there and then? That had been a perfect opportunity to come clean, to let him know that because of a decision she'd made long ago, she couldn't be pregnant.

She'd come close. It had been at the tip of her tongue, but her fear of losing him, coupled with the fact that it was his special day, had stopped her. Years ago, he'd found his mother cheating on his birthday. She didn't want it to also be associated with a break up, convinced that whenever she told him about her secret, she'd have to leave.

She couldn't bear the thought of roping him into a relationship knowing she wouldn't be able to give him the family that he longed for. Not in the typical way. Even if he wanted to stay with her, she wouldn't let him. He deserved to have everything he desired for his future.

Though it meant that her heart would shatter into pieces, she'd have to let him go. Tears filled her eyes at the thought of not being with Yomi. It had been way easier to display anger at him in the kitchen than to show her true dread—a life without him in it, or a life with him forced to accept her shortcomings.

To think that before she had met him, she'd been living with a man for five years—engaged to him for two—yet, his departure hadn't broken her. However, the mere idea of Yomi's absence made her feel sick to her stomach. How could one man change her life in such a short space of time?

"There are other ways to have children, Emem."

Natalie's words came back to her, causing a jolt of hope to flicker in her chest. She stiffened. After she'd been informed by the gynaecologist that she couldn't physically carry a pregnancy, she'd gone into a daze as the doctor had droned on about other ways she could be a mother.

Devastated, she hadn't taken anything in. And Ejike, who had sat beside her stoically, hadn't made any move to gather more information or book a follow-up appointment, so she had not really thought about it since then.

Now, as she lay beside the man who she'd go an extra mile for, the possibilities flooded her mind. She could make an appointment with Dr. Omogbai and find out more about what he'd been trying to tell her. She still had his number.

Her heart rate escalated as she ruminated more about these options. Of course, any one of them would be expensive, but she had some money saved up. And if Yomi was willing to pitch in ...

She stifled that thought. One step at a time. First things first. She'd gather all the information she needed including specialists and costs, then open up to him about everything, give him time to digest the news. Maybe then, with all the options laid out clearly when she broke the news, they'd be able to make the right decision together.

Four days later, Emem sat in front of Dr. Omogbai, her heart thumping as he settled in the seat opposite her.

"Emem, I am glad you're back here. You look much brighter. Happier. Two years ago, you seemed very ... distraught," he said, rolling a pen in his fingers.

"Thank you, Doctor. I am," she murmured, gaze focused on the oversized spectacles almost covering half of his face.

The previous time she'd been here, she hadn't taken much time to notice anything about him except the sadness in his eyes whilst he delivered bad news to her. But now, she could see that he wasn't the ogre who she'd thought him to be—the man that destroyed her chances of having a baby to save her life—but a kind, middle-aged doctor with concern for his patients.

"From your telephone call, you mentioned that you wanted to talk about starting a family. Is that still the case?"

"Yes, I'm here to discuss my options."

He flicked through his notes and then raised his eyes to meet hers.

"You also mentioned a partner. Isn't he coming?"

"He doesn't know yet that I can't have children naturally. I just want to ... to find out what avenues are available first before I tell him."

"It's always better to discuss these issues together ..."

"I know, Doctor ... I'm just not sure I want to bring him into my mess if I don't know all the facts about this first."

Dr. Omogbai remained silent for seconds, then lowered his pen onto his notes. "I understand the anxiety you have about telling your significant other about something as difficult as this. But now, there are many ways to be a mother. And they are not as farfetched as a lot of people believe."

He leaned forward. "It's always easier if the couple are committed together. However, I'll discuss the details with you today. You can always come back with him at other appointments."

"Thank you, Dr. Omogbai."

"Great," he said, opening the file in his hands.

Sitting still, Emem listened with rapt attention as the doctor spoke, showing her a presentation from his portfolio.

CHAPTER TWENTY-ONE

Yomi grinned as he stirred the pot of soup on the cooker in front of him. The tantalising aroma of boiling herbs and spices rose to his nose, and he dragged in a slow breath. He lifted the wooden ladle from the pot, swiped it on his palm, and then flicked his tongue over the green broth.

"Excellent," he sighed with self-appreciation.

He couldn't wait to bring Emem to her knees when she tasted the best *ewedu* soup ever, even if he did say so himself.

She'd cooked for him every time they'd had a homemade meal together. This time, he'd decided to treat her to a traditional soup he had honed down to perfection.

Satisfied with the final taste, he twisted the knob of the gas cooker and turned it off. Moving over to the kitchen sink, he began the task of washing all the utensils he'd used for cooking.

As he lifted a small bowl from the dirty pile, he heard a knock on the door and froze. He was in Emem's apartment and wasn't expecting her back just yet. She and Natalie had left only about forty-five minutes ago intending to spend the entire Saturday afternoon shopping for Natalie's wedding items. They couldn't possibly be back yet, considering they hadn't even agreed on the shop to patronise while they had been at the apartment strategizing their hunt.

The loud knock on the door came again. He sighed as he turned off the tap. He wiped his hands on the towel hooked to the wall and exited the kitchen, wondering who on Earth it could be. Maybe just a lost person seeking directions. He'd had his fair share of people knocking on his door at random times of the day, enquiring about a neighbour and sometimes even requesting to leave a parcel or message for one of the other occupants of the building.

"Who is it?" he asked by the door.

"I'm looking for Emem Akpan," a male voice declared.

Yomi twisted his lips in annoyance. *That's not the answer to my question, mate.* "And? Who are you?"

The person hesitated. "I should be asking you that. I'm her fiancé, Ejike."

Yomi froze. Ejike—the asshole ex Emem had told him about. She'd told him what the rotten bastard had done to her—run off to marry someone else in America. Why in the world would he think they were still engaged? What a loser.

"She's not around," he barked, fighting back the venom that rose to his throat.

"Well, let me see for myself."

Fuming, he unlocked the door and stepped out. "Who the hell do you think you are, showing up unannounced to her apartment?"

"Like I said, I'm Ejike. And who are you to tell me that my fiancée isn't around? This is her apartment, isn't it?" Ejike gave him a baleful once over and twisted his lips. "Are you her house boy?"

Rage, like Yomi had never felt before, erupted inside him, making him clench both fists, two seconds from punching this asshole in the face.

"As a matter of fact, I'm her boyfriend," he snarled, the strain in his arms almost painful from the effort of suppressing the need to swing his hands forward in attack. "And you are her ex-fiancé. She has nothing to say to you, so you may as well get moving and forget her."

Ejike stared at him, appearing dumbfounded for moments, and then threw his head back, laughing. The howling sound of his laughter grated on Yomi's nerves so much that he turned away abruptly, a final attempt to prevent himself from ramming his fist into Ejike's face.

"Tell Emem I'll be back…"

Yomi whirled back in a puff of rage. "I'm not telling her shit."

"A boy!" Ejike said, still chuckling. "Emem is trying to get back at me by fucking a boy—"

Yomi lurched forward and landed a heavy blow across Ejike's jaw, cutting him off and making him stagger backwards.

"Don't ever talk about Emem like that again!" he thundered, throwing another blow at Ejike that struck him on the shoulder.

With agility, Ejike pounced forward, pushing Yomi down with his weight.

"You think she's with you because she cares about you," Ejike growled, raising his fists and swinging downwards.

Yomi caught his wrist and held on, despite being trapped under the bulk of his heavy frame.

"Yes, she is, asshole. You bastard. How dare you come back to see her after what you did to her?"

"Did to her?" Ejike seethed, struggling to get his wrist out of Yomi's firm grip. "I married that American girl because I wanted to secure a green card for Emem and me—for our future."

"Get the fuck off me, fatso," Yomi barked. "You think I was born yesterday. I don't know what she ever saw in you."

Ejike bounded off Yomi with a low, harsh laugh. "I don't know what she sees in you, either. A small boy like you," he spat back. "Just tell her to come back home where she belongs. I'm the only one who'll still have her after what happened ..."

Ejike turned to leave, but something made Yomi snap. He jumped off the floor, not wanting the other man to have the last word.

"After what happened?" he yelled, his heart pounding, adrenaline pumping through his blood vessels.

Ejike swivelled back, a superior glint in his eyes.

"Oh, she hasn't told you ..." He snorted out a short laugh, turning away again. "I knew it! She can't be serious about you."

A perverse and almost uncontrollable need to lash out at the gigantic man with a receding hairline and arrogant bearing made Yomi tremble.

"Oh, she certainly is serious enough to wear my engagement ring around town," he lied, succumbing to the pettiness that he'd tried to suppress.

Profound satisfaction gripped him at the startled grunt that emitted from Ejike.

"Lies!" Ejike hissed, swirling back to face him again. "So, you want her so much that you'd forgo the fact that she can't have children? That she has no womb?"

Ejike's question held a heavy dose of spite, but also a touch of astonishment. Like he couldn't believe it.

Yomi's confidence shook, intense shock spiralling down his spine, leaving him stock-still.

"Now, you're lying—"

Ejike interrupted him with a loud snicker.

"Oh, so you're engaged to a woman without knowing that vital information about her!" He shook his head and stepped back. "You're more naïve than I thought," Ejike muttered as he turned away, strutting towards the front door, a self-assured spring in his step.

This time, Yomi remained motionless as he watched him leave, too startled to stop him.

"Tell Emem to come back home to the man that knows everything about her and still wants to be with her," Ejike tossed over his shoulder haughtily before he opened the door and strolled out, leaving Yomi standing in the narrow hallway, trembling, his stomach churning with despair and disillusionment.

***

Whistling softly, Emem slammed the door of her car and secured the lock to the vehicle, elated by the successful turn of events today. A smile spread across her lips as she opened the front door of the apartment building.

Her trip to the gynaecologist's clinic with Natalie this afternoon had brought so much hope. After a pelvic ultrasound performed by the doctor, she'd discovered that she still had viable eggs in her ovaries. She could have children with the surrogacy options available. And the amazing thing about the fantastic news included the reasonable cost of the procedure.

The hospital had offered her a sensible instalment payment plan that she could afford on her own salary without even needing Yomi's financial assistance.

She dragged in a breath, guilt overwhelming her that she'd not been completely honest with him about her whereabouts today. Indeed, she had gone shopping with her friend for an hour, but the main reason for leaving the apartment had been to honour the appointment with the specialist Dr. Omogbai had referred her to.

Well, today, she'd come clean and tell Yomi everything. Now that she knew there was hope for both of them, it would be easier baring her soul to him. Hopefully, he'd understand and accept her reason for holding back the truth from him. She would let him know that if he wanted, they could have it all. Including the family he desired.

She no longer had any reason to hold back from him. They could work it out together if he still chose to be with her in spite of the challenges ahead of them.

With a smile still splayed across her lips, she fished out the keys to her apartment. She'd texted Yomi twice while out, but he hadn't responded. She'd wondered why briefly and had almost panicked, wanting to ring him, when she'd stopped herself from acting like a stalking mother. He was probably resting on the sofa, binging on his favourite TV shows or watching football like he did on Saturday afternoons.

Emem slipped the key into the lock. God, it was good to be home. She pushed open the door and stopped dead in her tracks. It was broad daylight outside. So, why was the flat shrouded in darkness? A shiver ran up her spine.

The curtains were pulled closed. Odd. She'd left Yomi in her apartment this morning with the drapes open. Had he left? Why? They'd planned to spend the evening here.

A movement on the couch grabbed her attention.

"Yomi?" she called out hesitantly.

No response.

Panic rose up in her throat like bile, threatening to choke her. Was there an intruder in her house? She needed to get out of here. With the stealth of a SWAT team on a special ops mission, she slid a foot backward. Then another.

"Going somewhere?"

She froze again, scared out of her wits. But wait. The voice. Yomi?

Emem flicked her eyes back in the direction of the couch, where the voice had come from. Yes, it was Yomi, sitting on the sofa, his back ramrod straight, his body stiff as a board. He was staring at the television. The features of his face were contorted, as if he watched a Greek tragedy. But the television screen was black. The room was silent. Eerie. Was he sick?

"Yomi, w-what's going on? Do you feel okay?" she sputtered, flicking on the light switch.

Without a word, he rose and unfolded his body to his full six-feet-two-inches. She'd always loved his tallness, his five-inch height advantage over her that made her feel safe and protected.

Except right now. Something in his stance worried her. So stiff, so indignant, so overbearing. It didn't frighten her, but it did worry her.

"Guess who came by this afternoon?" he asked, his eyes bright with accusation.

"Yomi, why are you looking at me like that?"

"I asked you a question, Emem—"

"What's going on?"

"Ejike came by with a lot to say about you."

Blood leached down her brain, making her feel lightheaded. She held onto the armrest of the nearest couch to steady her feet and then took a step towards him. He jerked back, a low growl emitting through clenched teeth.

"Don't ..." he muttered.

"Yomi ..." She halted her advancement, a desperate plea in her voice.

"Don't." He pinned her with a broken look in his eyes. "Why didn't you tell me? I told you I love you. I told you everything about myself. The good, the bad, and the ugly. I trusted you with every secret of mine, yet..."

He trailed off, breathing heavily, his chest wall moving up and down. His Adam's apple bobbed as he swallowed, the muscles of his jaw tight, clearly fighting back intense emotions.

"You kept a very important aspect of your life from me. Crucial information that I had to find out from your ex in the hallway... you know, about him being the only man that can accept that you're unable to have children ..."

Emem's heart sank. Trepidation coiled inside her tummy like a snake crushing its prey. "Yomi, please sit down and listen ..."

"No! I'll stand," he barked. "Am I a joke to you? A young boy to screw and play about with? A bloody dildo for your amusement?"

"No, Yomi," she whispered, gradual panic setting in. She'd never seen him this angry. His face was contorted in a grimace, his feet spread apart, nostrils flaring with the sound of his heavy breathing. "I wanted to tell you, I was scared of losing you, of driving you away—"

His mirthless laughter interrupted her.

"Scared of telling me?" He shook his head. "And to think I have been hoping, praying that I knocked you up last time we ... and there I was, talking about making babies ...you must've been having a good laugh at my expense all this time."

"No, Yomi, I just didn't know how to start the conversation. It has been very hard for me ..."

"Hard for you?" He spat out his question, incredulity in his eyes. "How the fuck do you think I feel now?"

"I'm sorry." Tears filled her eyes. She darted forward and reached for him. "I'm sorry."

"Your tears won't cut it this time," he snarled, backing away abruptly, almost stumbling in his effort to evade her touch. "I'm done. Done! Don't you come anywhere near me ever again."

"Yomi, please ... please ..."

"And to think that I'd have stayed, no matter what. I'd have moved the heavens for you ..." His lowered tone, drenched in grief and defeat, pierced her heart. "But you didn't trust me enough to give me the chance to prove how much I love you."

With that statement hanging between them, he stepped aside and marched out of her apartment and out of her life.

Emem sank onto the floor, sobbing.

"I'm sorry, Yomi," she wailed. "I'm so sorry."

CHAPTER TWENTY-TWO

Yomi dashed out of Emem's apartment, his head spinning around in random circles. Almost running, he made his way to his flat, picked his car keys off the centre table, and scurried out of the building in a rush, needing to be as far away from her as possible.

How could she lie to him, keep something that earth-shattering from him? How could she? They'd been together for nearly two months. She knew how he felt about her. Didn't she think he'd need the information?

He jumped into his car and drove out of the estate in a daze, not sure of his intended destination. He just wanted to float away in the traffic of Lagos, forget that he'd laid his heart bare for the first time in his life, to a woman who didn't even consider him worthy of her future.

Without really pondering his intent, he found himself driving towards Ikeja to confront another woman who had let him down. He wasn't even sure what he wanted to say to her.

In less than an hour, he brought his car to a halt in the car park of *Selfridge Hotel*. Full of steam and indignation, he leapt out, enabled the vehicle security, and jogged towards the entrance, barely taking in the people who milled around in the sunshine.

The cool air inside the hotel blew against his face, a dramatic contrast to the biting heat outside that he'd just escaped. However, that did nothing to calm the turmoil boiling inside him. He needed to talk to his mother. Get some things off his chest.

Taking a deep breath in, he approached one of the free attendants by the large front desk.

"I'm here to see Mrs. Oladipo. Do you know what room she's in?" His mother had kept her last name after the divorce.

"I'm sorry. We don't divulge information about our guests," the slender man said, shaking his head regretfully.

Yomi sighed, retreating. He should have known better. He stepped aside, pulled his mobile phone from the pocket of his denim trousers, and sent a quick text to Kunle.

Seconds later, his phone beeped with the information he needed. With more confidence, he approached another receptionist, because the man who'd attended to him earlier was otherwise engaged in conversation with an elderly woman.

"Please, can you let Mrs. Oladipo in Room 524 know that Yomi is waiting at the lobby for her?"

The young woman smiled.

"Yes, of course, sir," she replied, typing into the computer in front of her. Her smile widened as she picked up the receiver beside her and lifted it to her ear.

"Good afternoon, Mrs. Oladipo. There's a Yomi here in the lobby. He'd like to see you." A brief pause. "Yes, light-skinned, dreadlocks ..."

Yomi's lips twitched. He didn't blame his mother for doubting the receptionist. He'd not sought her out for over ten years, avoiding her whenever she visited Nigeria, and purposely keeping her in the dark when he took a trip to London.

"She said you could come right up," the receptionist said as soon as she hung up. "The closest elevator is at the end of the hall to your left."

Yomi smiled in appreciation as he walked away. In less than five minutes, he found himself in front of his mother's room, nervous and feeling foolish for the impromptu visit. He blew out a short breath and tapped on the door.

Within seconds, the door opened, and his mother stood in front of him, dressed in a colourful boubou, her blond hair packed into a severe knot. She was beautiful—beautiful and delicate. Small in size and slender, she possessed a flawless olive skin tone from her Italian heritage, piercing blue eyes, and strikingly defined facial features. People had repeatedly told him that they looked exactly alike, but for many years, that observation had constantly irritated him.

"This is a pleasant surprise, Yomi," she said, snagging his attention back. She stepped away from the door. "Do come in."

He hesitated for seconds and then strolled into the room.

"Please have a seat," she said.

He didn't. Instead, he swept his gaze around, taking in the rumpled bed. It looked as if she'd been sleeping when he'd arrived. The moderate-size television, mounted on the wall and tuned to an international news station, was muted.

Not saying anything, he strolled over to the bedside table and lifted the framed photograph of his mother and the boy she'd married. The one he'd caught her with.

"He looks a lot older than …" he broke off.

"He's thirty-seven now, Yomi."

"Still … Mum …" He heard his mother's sigh and turned towards her. "Was it about sex?"

"No."

A direct answer. But not much else. He needed more.

He sucked his teeth and shrugged. "Then make me understand … I don't get it."

His mother smoothed a palm down the side of her gown, her fingers visibly trembling. "Would you like a drink before we talk?"

He nodded and waited in silence as she pulled out a bottle of white wine from the minibar.

"This is the most decent one in here," she said, referring to the bottle in her hands. "Sit, and let me get cups."

She moved over to the tiny cupboard by her bed and retrieved two transparent cups. Yomi took the bottle from her, uncorked it, and filled their cups half way. He settled in the sofa opposite the bed and lowered the bottle on the table beside him.

Holding her cup, his mother sat on the bed in front of him. She took a sip and smiled. "Not as bad as I imagined."

Yomi sipped his own drink and scrunched up his face.

"Bloody hot. What percent alcohol ..." He grabbed the bottle and peered at it. "Eighteen percent! Damn, Nigerians do have a high alcohol tolerance."

His mother laughed. "True, true. Even the Irish would be impressed."

His lips lifted into a smile. They fell silent, nursing their drinks for moments.

"Yomi, your father and I ... we didn't expect things to turn out the way they did," she began. The plastic cup in her hand squeaked from the force of her grip. "When we met, he was doing a Master's degree in London. We fell madly in love and were married in less than two months."

She cracked a reminiscent smile. "Back then, your father had the most beautiful eyes. And a way of making me feel like I was the only one in a room whenever we were together. He's a great man, Dele is. A wonderful man."

Yomi held his breath, still not getting her. He already knew his father to be a good and hardworking man. But that didn't explain why his mother, who thought the same, had cheated on and lied to him—her husband who loved her dearly.

"The plan was for us to live in London, raise our family together. He'd already brought your brother Segun from Nigeria to stay with us, so I was delighted," she continued, tracing her finger over the floral pattern on her gown.

"But nine years into our marriage, your father became restless, wanted to move back to Nigeria to begin an architectural business. That was all he could talk about then. After a lot of deliberation, we decided to relocate."

A slight flash of pain crossed her eyes. "But your father changed his mind at the last minute. He became worried about our safety. There had been too many political disruptions in the Nigerian government. We finally decided that it was better for him to move back alone while the rest of the family stayed in London. It was a simple plan. He'd visit as often as he could, and we'd remain a family."

Yomi remembered the moment when his father had waved goodbye to them on a foggy cold evening, before disappearing into the departure terminal of Heathrow airport. He had been only twelve at the time, but he could still recall the melancholy that had fallen on everyone as he'd walked away.

Her soft sigh brought his mind back to the present.

"We tried to make it work. For years, he shuffled between London and Lagos. But as the years went by, we began to drift apart."

The ends of her lips drooped slightly. And for the first time, he noticed the tiny wrinkles at the corners of her mouth, showing a hint of her age.

At fifty-four, she could pass for someone more than ten years younger. But tonight, as she recounted the breakdown of her marriage, she appeared a lot older to him. Like a mother—not the disturbing image he'd fought of her in his mind, the vixen he'd caught having sex on the couch.

"I asked him for a divorce, but he begged me to stay. He worried about disrupting Segun's life once again. You know how close Segun and I were."

Yomi nodded. His mother and Segun had a tight bond. She'd been a perfect stepmother to him.

"I agreed. And we also agreed to have an open marriage."

Yomi stiffened, the announcement from his mother difficult to digest.

"Your father knew about Ronald, Yomi. He understood. I was alone most of the time with three young children while he was always away, chasing one architectural high or another. I'm a woman, Yomi. I have needs ..."

He cringed inwardly, not wanting to hear that, but held spellbound by this revelation. His parents' divorce had been messy, with bitter words thrown back and forth between them. And he had always assumed that his father had been devastated by the affair. He had no clue that not only had his father been aware, he'd also signed off on it.

"Your dad told me that as long as nobody else knew, I could carry on my affair with Ronald. He, too, had someone in Nigeria. He never mentioned her, and I never asked."

Yomi's jaw dropped, disbelief snatching his breath away. His mother nodded vigorously as she raised her cup to her lips. She took a quick sip.

"When you walked in on me and Ronald, that deal with your father disintegrated. That was my mistake.

He never wanted you, or anyone else, for that matter, to know the truth about our marriage arrangement."

Her tone became low, a soft reflective tinge in her eyes. Something in his heart tugged as he eyed his mother. With her shoulders slouched and lips thinned into taut lines, she looked like a woman full of regrets.

"A part of me wonders if I became more reckless with Ronald because I wanted someone to find out about us. I got tired of living the double life. I wanted my freedom to be with the man who had slowly become a vital part of my life. I wanted Ronald."

Yomi sipped his drink quietly, mulling over her words, trying to come to grips with the fact that because he'd misunderstood the situation, he had lost so many years with his mother.

"Yomi, I never meant to hurt you or your father. But after all is said and done, there is a part of me that's not sorry. I deserved better—to be free to pursue my happiness." Her solemn confession drew him from his roving thoughts. "Apart from being a mother and a wife, I'm also a woman. Ronald loves me like a woman."

"Okay, Mum!" he shrieked, lifting his hand in protest. "Don't want to hear any more about you and your super-lover, Ronald."

He rolled his eyes, and she smiled in response.

"I promise not to talk about him if you promise to forgive me."

Yomi raised his drink in salute to her. "Deal."

Her resultant smile as she reciprocated the gesture made his heart swell with joy. Finally, they could put the past behind them and move on.

"And Yomi ..." She stretched her arms across the bed, reached for a polythene bag, and pulled out a small gift-wrapped box. He recognised it. It was her birthday gift to him that he'd deliberately snubbed. "Your father sent this back to me. But I want you to have it."

She tossed it to him, and he caught it deftly in his free hand. Lowering his plastic cup onto the table beside him, he unwrapped the package and smiled.

A framed photograph of him as a beaming six-year-old sitting on his mother's knee. He remembered when this picture had been taken. The day he'd brought back the trophy for best artist in a painting competition. She'd been so proud of him.

Nostalgic emotions swelled in his chest.

"I want you to remember that you'll always be that Yomi to me—my son whom I love dearly and I'm so proud of."

He swallowed hard.

"Thanks, Mum," he said, brushing his thumb across the surface of the picture. "Thank you."

She nodded, a pleased grin on her face.

Silence followed. The air conditioner droned in the room like the peeving hum of mosquitoes trapped in a net. Although streaks of the late afternoon sun rays pierced through the drapes, the room maintained a dark and cosy feel to it, belying the bright, summery weather outside.

"So, Yomi, what happened?"

His mother's question broke the silence.

"What do you mean?"

"You're my son. And despite our time apart, I know you well enough to confidently assume that something or someone pushed you to come unannounced to see me."

He stiffened, surprised by her accurate deduction. Yet, somewhat saddened that he'd missed many years of this—being able to talk to her whenever he wanted.

"You can tell me," she pressed, her soft voice soothing and encouraging. "I'll only listen and not give my opinions if you don't want them."

"I'm in love with a woman who can't have children," he said baldly, then chiding himself inwardly for his bluntness, he corrected, "Who has reproductive ... challenges ..."

His mother didn't say anything for moments, her eyes trained on him.

"Emem? The woman you were with at your birthday dinner?" she asked finally.

Yomi nodded. He dragged in a regretful breath. "I just found out today. Her ex came by unexpectedly and dropped that bombshell news before he strolled out cockily."

"Oh, that's rough ..."

"I hate that she lied to me, you know. Kept something as serious as that from me, knowing how much I love her."

His mother gazed at him, absentmindedly twisting her now empty cup in her hands.

"I'm so confused, Mum. I want to be with her, but a part of me wonders if I can live a live without having children."

"What exactly is the problem with her fertility?"

"I'm not sure. Her ex said something about her not having a womb. I was too angry to find out more details from her. I broke it off with her and stormed off."

His mother sighed. She rose from the bed, walked over to him, and settled on the armrest of his sofa.

"Yomi, things are not always simple, neat, black or white," she said, draping an arm around his shoulders. "Life is messy, baffling, grey ... With any woman you'd ever fall for, there would be challenges.

The most important question to ask yourself is whether she is worth going through them with."

"But she lied to me, Mum, never gave me a chance to make my own decision about this."

"I agree that she should have told you about her fertility issues. But have you asked yourself or asked her why she kept things from you? Do you know the details of her struggle, her pain? And have you ever thought about what it must feel like disclosing something as difficult as that to someone you care about?"

He ground his jaw, conflicted as he recalled the fear in Emem's eyes when she'd finally been confronted with the truth. She'd admitted being worried about losing him by telling him, and he'd done exactly what she'd been anxious about—left her without a backward glance.

"Yomi, children are a blessing. And I'm thrilled to have three of my own. But one's place in life is so much more than parenthood. There are too many unhappy parents in this world."

His mother paused, her eyes distant and pained, as though recollecting unpleasant events of the past. He knew that she'd been adopted, having been rescued from her abusive mother and a barely present father.

"Besides, there are several ways to be a parent—surrogacy, adoption, fostering ... so many ways. If you want Emem in your life, is her inability to get pregnant the deal breaker? Would you rather be an unhappy biological father or a happy adoptive father?"

"Oh, Mum, I didn't even get a chance to think." He raked his palm over his face in frustration. "I suppose the fact that her ex knew, and I didn't, made me so jealous that I became angry with her."

"Jealousy ... ah, a powerful emotion." A small smile curved her lips. Drawing him closer, she planted a soft kiss to the side of his forehead. "Yomi, do you love Emem? Is she worth trips to adoption agencies, fertility clinics, surrogacy centres, or even not having children? These are your options with her. If the answer is yes, then by all means go for her."

Silence fell between them as he considered his mother's advice. Of course, Emem was worth it all. He'd never felt about any other woman the way he did for her. She brightened up his day, challenged him to be better, made him laugh. Most of all, she loved him. He could tell that she did.

Although he'd always imagined children as a part of his life, he could always go with the flow, see what the future had in store for him, for them. As long as he had Emem by his side, they'd be okay.

"Yes, Mum. Emem is worth it all," he said, finally, relief flooding his senses for the first time since he'd been confronted by Emem's ex. "The question now is, does she think I'm worth it?"

"Well, my wonderful son, you'll have to find that out on your own."

CHAPTER TWENTY-THREE

Emem sat in a recliner on the balcony of Natalie's apartment, gaze glued to a woman standing in the street below. On the woman's head rested a large water container. A baby—possibly sleeping—lay strapped onto her back, while she held smaller gallons of water in each hand.

From the way her eyes darted around, Emem guessed she was waiting for a taxi or some other mode of transportation.

She found herself enthralled by the sheer resilient way the woman bore her burdens, her face hopeful, her posture sure. This routine probably wasn't alien to her. She most likely left her home every day to fetch clean water for daily use from one of the public taps located in affluent areas such as this. A practical and necessary task for survival.

Women like her didn't have time to wallow, or cry like she'd been doing for the past three days. They simply got on with life, kept pushing despite any drawbacks the universe threw at them.

"Emem, you have to stop crying."

Natalie's voice brought her mind back from her distant thoughts. She turned sideways and regarded her friend who was seated on a similar recliner beside her.

"I know," she whispered, wiping the tears on her cheeks with the back of her hand.

"Why don't you call Yomi? You guys can work things out."

She shook her head as she pulled a tissue from the box resting on her knee.

"I don't think so." She dabbed her eyes and blew her nose noisily. "I mean, I love and miss him. But I think it's best that we split. Yomi deserves a family without all the stress ..."

"Come on, Emem, you can't keep saying that," Natalie said, her brows crinkled together in concern. "What about what you deserve? He may have calmed down and want to work things out with you?" She puffed out a sigh. "Emem, put your SIM card back into your phone and call Yomi ... try to explain."

"I have to let him go, Natalie."

She had thought hard and long since she'd packed her belongings in a hurry from her apartment to stay with her friend. Sometimes, love meant setting someone free. Especially when the person would be better off. It hurt, but she had to stay strong.

"No, you don't, unless you've told him everything from your point of view." Natalie lifted the mobile device from the tea table between them and held it out to her. "Switch on your phone, dear. Yomi may even be trying to call you."

Emem took it from her but set it on the floor beside her.

"I won't switch it on, because if I do, I'll be tempted to call Yomi. I am determined to set him free. Not drag him into my mess again." She paused, raking her fingers through the short curls of her hair. "Besides, I turned it off to keep that asshole, Ejike, from blowing up my phone. He now has this number after I called him telling him to go to Hell."

"The audacity of that fool, showing up to your apartment unannounced!"

Natalie's shrill voice, full of disdain, pleased Emem. She loved that her friend always had her back. She was that friend who one could call up at two in the morning to be the designated driver after a drunken night out. And she could always be counted on never to sugar-coat anything. Honest to a fault, Natalie gave her points of view without holding back.

"I mean, after months of being incommunicado, he tracks me down to cause *wahala* in my life," Emem muttered, renewed rage building in her chest. "I was so angry when I found out someone at the radio station gave him my address."

"How inappropriate!" Natalie exclaimed.

"Exactly! I've warned them to never ever give out my personal information without my consent."

If they hadn't, she would have broken the news gently to Yomi, and he may have received it better.

Instead, she'd been on the defensive. She didn't even blame Yomi for his reaction. She, too, would have been angry if any of his ex-girlfriends had confronted her to divulge his secrets. Ejike had no right to do what he did. None whatsoever.

"And when I called the idiot earlier, he had the nerve to try and explain away getting married to another woman. Green card, my ass!"

Natalie hissed loudly. "What a goat. Thinking we are fools. He expects you to believe that it was for your own good that he cheated on you."

"As if I ever talked about moving to America. He was the one obsessed with the idea, not me."

"Don't mind him, *jare*. Just block his number."

"I did. But he kept calling me with other numbers. That's why I have to change mine." Fresh tears welled up in her eyes. "I wonder what he even wants from me. He has won. He gets the wife, the baby, and the life he's always wanted, while I'm sitting here damaged and alone ..."

Natalie covered Emem's hand with hers.

"You aren't damaged, my dear," she whispered in a soothing voice. "And you are most certainly not alone. No matter what, I'm here for you, and it will all be okay."

"Thank you," she choked out, reaching for another tissue.

Silence settled between the friends as they gazed out into the streets below. Emem inhaled slowly as she swiped the tissue over her eyes. The woman she'd sighted earlier was no longer there, and for some odd reason, her absence comforted Emem. Life carried on. Despite how gloomy she felt now, someday, she would move on, too.

Natalie's phone buzzed loudly—a rap song with an upbeat tone that shattered the melancholic mood. Natalie glanced at the screen suspiciously, letting it ring for moments until it stopped.

Emem raised both brows in question.

"Unknown number," she mouthed in response.

The phone began to ring again.

"Pick it up."

Natalie shook her head. "Could be those callers that burst into Hausa language as soon as you answer, not bothering to find out who's on the other end."

Emem chuckled. She'd also received many of those calls, and despite managing to apply her network's call-blocking procedures, a few managed to get through.

The ringing fizzled out, and they both heaved a relieved breath. A temporary respite, because, seconds later, it began again.

Sighing in frustration, Natalie slid her thumb across the screen and rested the phone against her ear.

"Who's this?" she snapped, rolling her eyes.

Emem noticed as Natalie's face changed from annoyance to surprise.

"Oh, Ini, how are you?"

Emem's eyes widened. She sat forward, knocking the box of tissues to the floor.

"I'm fine, thanks." Natalie's gaze darted to her. "And yes, she's here. Her phone is off ..." Seconds of chattering from the other end of the line, then Natalie's voice. "Long story ... is everything okay?"

Natalie nodded repeatedly as she listened to the response to her question. "Great. Cool. Nice to hear from you, too. I'll hand the phone over."

She held out the handset to Emem.

Fingers trembling, Emem took the phone from Natalie and placed it over her ear. She hardly ever heard from her sister. In fact, they were so distant from each other that they spoke maybe three or four times a year—during birthdays and holidays. Something had to be wrong.

"Hi, Ini," she said, heart thundering inside her ribcage.

"Hey, sis," Ini said, her hesitant tone immediately worrying.

"Everything okay?" Emem asked, palms sweating and pulse rate amped up. She couldn't stomach more bad news. Not this week. "Dad? Mum?"

"Yes, everything's fine." Ini hesitated, drawing in a ragged breath. The harsh sound prickled Emem's ear. "Okay, not really ... Dad has been diagnosed with type two diabetes."

Emem let out a sigh of relief. Okay, it wasn't cancer, a terminal disease or death ... but still, she waited in silence, convinced there was more to the news.

"He ... He was diagnosed two years ago. But he hasn't been taking his medications, and now, he has a deep leg ulcer."

"What!" Emem sucked in a breath. "Why hasn't he been taking his medications? What's going on?"

Her sister didn't say anything for long moments. And a slow burn rose up her gut, almost choking her.

She didn't need Ini's answer. She already knew why—because of his faith.

Their father believed in divine healing—that doctors and medications weren't God's plan. She'd grown up hearing him tell his congregants that anyone who died from an illness didn't have enough faith—'Thou shalt not die ... Your faith has made you whole ... Trust in the Lord with all thine heart.' Just a few of the Bible passages he'd guilted his church members with, to prevent them from seeking medical attention when sick.

"Please, Emem, I would like you to come and talk to him." Ini's solemn entreaty brought her mind back to the present. "He isn't listening to anyone."

"Why me? He never listened to me, either."

"Well, you're the only one who can challenge him without any religious sentiment involved, since ..." Her sister trailed off.

"Since I'm a sinner who doesn't believe ..."

"I didn't say that."

"Well, you didn't need to. You've always judged me, thought me to be the evil witch."

"And so have you, Emem. You've judged me, too."

She twisted her lips, confused at the angry pronouncement from her sister.

"How? How have I ever judged you? When all I ever did was try to help—"

"Who says I needed help, Emem?" her sister interjected, her tone sharp with annoyance. "For your information, I love being a Christian. I love the fact that I fast and pray, and go to church, and obey my parents. I wasn't forced. I didn't need saving from Dad or the church. I enjoy it all. We all did. Except you thought we were being bullied by Dad and Mum to believe, for our faith."

Moments of silence followed. Emem ground her jaw. Her sister's bitter accusation scorched her. Was that really how she'd treated Ini and the rest of the family? As if she were smarter, superior? As if she knew more, had all the answers?

She massaged her temples to ease up the tension building in her head. She hadn't anticipated this soul-baring session today. "So why are you calling me? Why do you need me to talk to Dad if that's all part of your enjoyable faith?"

"I'm calling because Daddy will die if he doesn't start his medications. He needs insulin," Ini answered. "And being stupid isn't part of my faith. The fact that Dad believes medicine is sinful doesn't mean I do, too. That has always been the problem between us, Emem. You never considered my individuality. You lumped me together with every Christian in the church."

She remained silent, her face warm, her throat tight with shame at the accurate assessment from her sister. Admittedly, her displeasure with the church had interfered with their relationship, and she had never tried hard enough to find out what Ini's personal beliefs were.

Maybe because Ini always looked so pious and subdued, never challenging their parents, covering her body with clothes from head to toe, just generally behaving like the rest of the people whom Emem had dubbed religious zombies with no personalities.

Thinking about it now, she agreed that she'd judged Ini, willing her to snap out of her shell, become more questioning of their religion. And for that, she felt remorse.

"It was never my intention—" she began solemnly.

"Water under the bridge, sis." Ini cut her off. "No apologies needed. God made all human temperaments different purposefully. There's a reason for your presence in our family."

And that reason is because Mum got pregnant for Dad. A smile tugged Emem's lips as she swallowed back the cynical response. Instead, she asked, "What does Mum have to say about Dad's refusal to take his medications?"

"She was the one who asked me to call you," she replied, her tone light and teasing. "Emem, we've always listened to your critical questions about the church, even though it appeared we didn't. Never think otherwise."

A flicker of joy settled in her chest. Maybe it was time to say goodbye to old resentments, try to bridge the gap between herself and her family.

"Ini, since we're being honest, I want to say that there's a part of me that envies your absolute faith in God, your resolute confidence in a power that you can't see or fully understand. I'm not wired that way."

"I can always convert you—"

"Nah, sis. Too many unanswered questions for me to believe."

"You never can tell what the future holds ..."

"That, I agree with," she said, a small smile splayed on her lips. She sucked her lower lip between her teeth, contemplating her final answer to her sister's initial request. "Okay, sis. I'll book the next available flight for tomorrow."

"Oh, thank you, Emem."

The relief in her sister's voice brought another smile to her face.

***

"I'm here to see Emem Akpan from Mainland FM, please," Yomi asked the middle-aged man standing by the gate.

The short and slender security guard dressed in a pale blue uniform gave him a baleful look, his eyes narrowed into annoyed slits.

"And you are?" An irate question in a gruff tone.

Neither offended Yomi. He totally got it. Anyone forced to stand in the piercing sun for hours on end, opening and closing a gate, couldn't possibly be welcoming.

"I'm Yomi Oladipo. Emem Akpan's ... friend. I need to speak to her." He flashed him a smile, hoping to charm his way into the compound of the building where Mainland FM's offices were situated.

"And is she expecting you?"

For a brief moment, he considered lying, anything to improve his chances of entry.

"No, she's not. But I'm here to discuss an urgent matter with her," he admitted, finally, deciding to be honest. The man looked like someone who would make things very difficult for anyone who crossed him.

"Urgent in what way?"

"*Oga*, sir." He changed tactics. Better to stroke the guard's ego. "It's for an important family matter. Please let me in, sir."

The man hesitated, glanced at the building and then back at him. "And what can you do for me?"

The nerve. Imagine a guard bribing people before letting them in? Ordinarily, Yomi would have used this as an opportunity to show his disdain for bribery, spent time pointing out the criminality of the corrupt act, and even gone ahead to report to the guard's superiors. But today, he actually saw it as good fortune—a chance to get inside the building.

He reached for his wallet and pulled out two thousand Naira.

"This is all I have," he said, struggling to keep his irritation from his tone.

"Ah, my *oga*!" The man grinned, exposing tobacco-stained teeth and a blackened tongue. "You should have told me you're one of us. Come on in and welcome." He pressed a remote, and the barrier by the gate slowly lifted. "It's the last building in the complex." He pointed to the end of the carpark. "Park your car there, sir."

Clenching his jaw tightly to prevent the snicker that almost made it past his mouth, Yomi stretched his lips into a tight smile and muttered a phoney thanks as he steered his vehicle inside the compound.

He couldn't afford to miss Emem today. When he'd returned from visiting his mother four days ago, he had been extremely disappointed to find her car absent from their apartment building's parking lot.

Assuming she had also gone out to clear her head, he'd decided to wait 'til the next day to go back and try reconciling with her, to tell her he loved her and wanted to work things out. However, to his dismay, her apartment door had still been locked the day after, and her vehicle remained absent from the compound.

He had gone from door to door, frantically knocking until one of her neighbours had informed him that she had seen Emem leaving her apartment crying and with a suitcase in her hand. Distraught by that information, he'd tried calling her number repeatedly to no avail, angry with himself that he neither had Natalie's phone number nor address.

This afternoon as he sat behind his desk at work, idly going through the new digital plans for a government building he had been assigned to design, an idea had come to him. He knew where Emem worked.

Galvanised by the thought, he had picked up his mobile phone, searched for the contact number for Mainland FM, and dialled. He'd managed to get through after thirty minutes of waiting on the phone, only to be told by the receptionist that she couldn't give out any personal information regarding anyone that worked in the station.

Not deterred by the roadblocks he'd come across in his attempt to contact Emem, he'd switched off his computer, cleared his work schedule, and left the office. Maybe a face-to-face approach would get her out of her hiding place. They needed to talk. He needed to let her know how much she meant to him, that having or not having children was secondary to their love for each other. He needed her back in his life. She belonged with him.

Yomi parked his SUV at the only empty spot available. He leapt out of the car and dashed towards the tall white three-story building. Mainland FM was at the top floor with the lower two belonging to other businesses.

He entered the corridor adjacent to a cable network agency on the ground floor. Darting his eyes round for moments, he searched for the nearest elevator. A satisfied sigh flew from his mouth when he spotted it on a corner. Heart beating with anticipation, he rushed over and pressed the up arrow button on the wall.

Minutes later, he was inside an empty elevator on his way to see Emem. His gut twisted with nervous anxiety. He hadn't even prepared a speech, not planned what to say. What if she didn't want to see him? What if—

The loud chime of the elevator interrupted his thoughts.

He took a deep breath in and stepped out, flashing a perfunctory smile at the two women waiting for the lift. He spotted the receptionist immediately. She was in a medium-sized cubicle at the end of a short hallway.

As he approached her, he quickly flicked his gaze to the glass window to check his reflection. In a navy blue business suit and red tie, and with his locks swept neatly away from his face, he looked too formal. Not the way he wanted Emem to see him. But he hadn't had time to change, and he frankly didn't care much about his appearance right now. All that occupied his mind was having Emem back in his life.

"Hello, I'm Yomi Oladipo," he said to the young receptionist at the desk. "I am here to see Emem Akpan."

She regarded him blankly for seconds.

"Good afternoon, sir," she said, glancing at the small computer screen. "I'm not aware that she is expecting anyone."

"She isn't expecting me," Yomi said quickly. "But I'd be grateful if you let her know I am around."

The receptionist smiled. "Okay, sir."

She lifted the small receiver by her desktop and dialled.

"Hi, Madam, this is Temi," she said into the phone, keeping her eyes on him as she spoke. "There's a Yomi Oladipo here to see Emem." He heard the chatter at the other end of the line while the receptionist nodded. "Okay, ma. Thanks."

"Emem is not in today," she said, replacing the phone to its cradle. "Her boss, Madam Nnenna, will be here in a second."

"Oh, thanks," he said.

Yomi's face fell. He tried to curtail his disappointment as he stepped aside to wait for Emem's boss to come down.

In less than ten minutes, a small, curvy woman strolled in. The woman nodded an acknowledgement at the receptionist, who in turn tipped her head in his direction.

He smiled as she walked over to him.

"Good afternoon, sir. I'm Nnenna," she greeted. "I work with Emem."

"Hello, Nnenna. Please call me Yomi," he replied, offering his hand to her for a handshake.

"Yomi." A smile curved her lips as she shook his hand. "Nice to finally meet you. I've heard a lot of good things about you."

His heart leapt with joy. He considered it a positive sign that Emem talked about him with her friends.

"Thank you. Pleased to meet you, too." He hesitated, trailed a finger over his jaw, and then sighed. "About Emem ... do you know how I can reach her? Her number isn't going through, and your receptionist said she isn't around."

"I am sorry, Yomi," Nnenna said ruefully. "We are not allowed to give out personal information about our staff."

"Please, at least tell me where she is ... why she isn't at work ... Is she okay?"

"I'm sorry, there is a confidentiality issue ..."

"Please, I need to speak to her." His tone became desperate. "I know she may be staying with Natalie, her friend. Do you know her?"

Nnenna nodded. Hope rose within him, and he inhaled sharply.

"Do you have her number? Please let me have it if you do. She isn't your staff, so no problem there." He spoke fast, not catching his breath between sentences, the renewed prospect of getting in touch with Emem exhilarating.

That seemed to give her pause. An impish smile spread slowly across her face.

"Hmmm... handsome and clever ..." Nnenna's eyes shone as she shoved her hand into the pocket of her red and yellow Ankara dress and retrieved her phone. "Lucky for you, I not only have Natalie's number, but she is also my friend. And we believe in you and Emem together. By all means, you can have it."

Intense relief surged through his senses, making him breathless. "Thanks so much. You can't imagine what this means to me."

"No worries. Go get your woman," she replied, still smiling. "All I ask is for you to always treat my girl right."

"I promise to try my very best," he said, his thumb hovering eagerly over the screen of his mobile phone as he prepared to input the phone number that would get him a step closer to hearing from Emem again.

CHAPTER TWENTY-FOUR

Butterflies flickered all over Emem's tummy as she sat in the back seat of a taxi on her way to the large estate where her parents lived. As always, this journey made her nervous. No matter how many times she tried to tell herself that as a grown woman, her parents' disappointment with her choices shouldn't matter, she knew it did. Somewhere deep inside her lay a need to be accepted for her own beliefs, her decisions, not cast away as the black sheep of the family.

Like all the times she'd visited home, she had stayed in a hotel last night, much to the disapproval of Ini, who had invited her over to her family home.

It wasn't that she didn't want to stay with her sister, not at all. Her reason for declining the invitation was because Ini's children, especially her six-year-old son, also shared the same curiosity Emem had had at that age.

Ubong had begun asking her questions about Christianity that she didn't want to answer. She knew it would piss her sister off if she told the truth about her own beliefs to Ini's son. To prevent being in that sort of conflict for prolonged periods, she always avoided staying too long with her sister's family.

She hated it, because in reality, she wanted to be the cool auntie who told lots of stories to her nephews and nieces, but her tales weren't from religious books or the Bible, which she knew Ini would prefer her kids hearing.

Sighing, she glanced out the rolled-up window. A typical rowdy view of Saturday afternoons in Port

Harcourt. Loud motorcycles carrying passengers filtered through the heavy traffic, honking horns from vehicles blared in the streets, and a dense cloud of exhaust smoke polluted the air.

It was quite unfortunate that the capital of the state responsible for production of crude oil, a major natural resource for the country, remained a poorly developed part of Nigeria. In fact, every time she came back home, it seemed the neglect had worsened, and the quality of infrastructures had diminished.

She shook her head. Although she sometimes missed Port Harcourt, Lagos had become her home. And with that thought, Yomi's image flashed through her mind. Being with him had also felt like home.

Deep regret formed like a thick wedge which suddenly lodged in her throat. She missed him so badly that it physically hurt. Last night, while lying on the bed in her hotel room, feeling lonely and miserable, a profound desire to ring him had overwhelmed her.

She had placed her former SIM card in her phone to find a cache of missed-call notifications and WhatsApp messages flooding her screen ... all from Yomi. She'd gone through the messages, cherishing each word as she read them over and over and over again.

'We need to talk, Emem, please pick up your phone.'

'I'm sorry. I miss you.'

'I love you, please call me.'

'Emem, why are you not responding? I thought we meant something to each other. ☺'

'Oh, I wish I knew Natalie's number or address.'

'Emem! Please!'

'I love you. I won't ever give up.'

That last text received a day ago had made her heart pound violently, luring her further to ring him. But she had resisted with every ounce of power within her and slipped the SIM card out of the phone again before throwing it into the bin. No need to tempt herself anymore. Then, she had realised that she knew Yomi's number by heart. The temptation could never really disappear, but she had to be resolute.

It didn't matter how much she loved and missed him—she had to let him go. He wanted children. And she couldn't be responsible for putting him through a life of uncertainty.

She had resolved that after her return to Lagos, she would set out on the quest to be a mother on her own, try the surrogacy route first, and if that didn't work, she'd adopt. Whatever it took, she'd do it on her own.

"Madam, where is your house?" her taxi driver asked, breaking through her musings.

To her utter delight, he had remained silent throughout the entire journey, leaving her to her thoughts.

"That one there." She pointed to the white mansion at the end of the narrow road where the car had pulled into.

The man's lips parted into a shocked gasp. "Are you related to Reverend Akpan?"

Emem chuckled.

"Yes," she answered. "The prodigal daughter."

The man's scrunched up his forehead in question.

"Long story," she muttered as she reached for her wallet and stepped out of the taxi.

After settling the fare, she strolled over to the gate and pressed the doorbell. Moments later, a small partition at the centre of the black gate slid open, and a face poked through.

"Ah, Madam. Welcome!" Zachariah exclaimed, a delighted grin splitting his face. The security officer, who had served the family for years, opened the gate immediately.

"Mr. Zackie!" Emem greeted him, bumping her knuckles against his—their special greeting. Many times, when she was younger, he had let her sneak out of the house without her parents knowing. She treasured his loyalty to her. "How are you? And your family?"

"Madam, the Madam. I'm doing well, thank God. And my last son is now in university studying law."

"Wow! Congratulations. Cosmos will make a great lawyer."

"Yes, o. I'm praying that he doesn't get distracted from his school work."

"I am sure he won't." She reached for her wallet, pulled out a wad of cash, and handed it to him. "For his fees."

"Thank you, Ma. God bless you," he said, bowing his head and rubbing his palms together in a show of gratitude.

"You're welcome, Mr. Zackie."

Emem scanned the compound. A fleet of six shiny cars were strategically parked inside the large space. She recognised her mother's Jeep and Ini's SUV, but all the others were new to her. She twisted her lips in a cynical smile. Ironic that her family's religious modesty wasn't reflected in their choice of material possessions.

As CEOs and shareholders of the successful Christian ministry, her parents and siblings lived exorbitant lifestyles in large mansions, driving expensive cars, and flying first class all over the world. Her father even had a bodyguard and was in talks to purchase a private jet. If that didn't contradict his usual message about God being his divine protector, she wondered what else could.

"The entire family is inside waiting, Ma. Welcome again," Zachariah said, bringing her mind back.

"Thanks," she whispered.

Sucking a slow breath in, she began her walk towards the front door of her family home.

***

The day was going better than expected. Two hours into the homecoming luncheon her father had arranged for her as he usually did, yet, she hadn't heard any speech by any member of her family about her sinful life in Lagos. To the contrary, they'd discussed other topics, including the last presidential election that had left the country divided.

Emem couldn't believe how much she was enjoying herself. Weird, but it seemed that the entire family had been replaced with imposters. And she was beginning to get suspicious.

"I will never again withhold my opinion about my preferred presidential candidate," her father who was at the reclining chair at the far end of the enormous sitting room said, lifting a bottle of water from the tea table beside him. "Lord knows, next time around, I'll use the pulpit to try and convince people to vote PDP."

"Dad, politics don't belong in the church." This came from Emem's younger brother, Udo, who was also a head pastor in the church.

"I think it should be," her father said. "There's nowhere in the Bible that condemns politics."

"Give to Caesar what is Caesar's, and to God what is God's—Mark 12:17," Udo said.

"Emem, what do you think?" asked her mother, seated beside her husband.

She blinked. How odd—for her mum to ask for an opinion about the Bible from her, about anything for that matter.

"I ... I think the church itself is based on politics. You can't separate politics from religion," she answered, rocking her sleeping nine-month-old niece in her arms.

"You are wise, my daughter," her mum said, shocking her even more. "And what do you also think about taking medicines when one is ill? Is it against the will of God? Or is it a reasonable idea?"

She caught the subtle looks her siblings exchanged and immediately understood what was happening. It suddenly dawned on her what the entire day had been all about. They had all connived to have an intervention for their father, and she was here to be the punching bag—the only person in the family, who like always, held strong anti-religious views.

As much as it annoyed her that she was being used as a pawn, she decided to go with the flow anyway. If this is what it took to get her father to accept treatment for his diabetes, so be it.

"I believe it is a reckless decision to abandon medicines that have been proven by science to cure illness."

"No!" her father huffed. "You can't place your trust in herbs and also want God's healing. The Bible says, you can't serve two masters."

"Nonsense, Dad." The baby in her arms stirred, then settled back into slumber, snuggling closer to her chest. "If you believe God created the world, then you should be accepting of medicines made from the earth. They are all part of God's work."

Her father opened his mouth as though about to refute her statement, glanced sideways at his wife, and then back at Emem.

"They told you about my diabetes," he said, his thick eyebrows angled together as annoyance shone in his eyes.

"Yes." She didn't bother to deny it. "You need insulin. And from what I've read about the condition, insulin is the final stage before severe complications set in."

Her father dragged in a ragged breath, but said nothing. The room remained tense, her siblings all silent, like they always were during any spat between her and their father about religious topics they disagreed on.

"You have a leg ulcer, Dad. Even though it's well-bandaged and tucked inside your trousers, we are all being too polite to tell you that we can smell the antiseptic used in dressing your wound. That in itself is medicine."

She rose, strolled over to the playpen at the corner of the sitting room, and lowered her niece gently onto it. Turning to her father, she looked him squarely in the face. "What are you trying to prove by refusing to take your medications? That you can't die? That you're immortal?" She shook her head. "Even Jesus died, Dad."

Her father hissed, tapping his fingers loudly on his armrest. A sign that her words were getting him riled up.

"Or are you afraid that taking your medications would make you eat the words you repeatedly spewed at your congregation from the altar, the guilt you made them feel for trusting in science?"

"Turn away from blasphemy and turn to Jesus," her father said through gritted teeth.

"Turn away from pride and humble yourself before the Lord," she retorted.

Silence. The charged atmosphere was almost palpable. Everyone else disappeared from her consciousness as her gaze zeroed on her father. His facial muscles tightened as he gripped his seat firmly for moments, his body hunched forward as though prepared to leap at her.

She remained standing, fearlessly holding her stance, refusing to cower to his intimidation.

With a sigh, he suddenly slumped back onto the recliner, a hollow look in his eyes. And for the first time, she realised his vulnerability. His need to always be upright and perfect had made him lose focus, forget his own humanity.

"Dad," she said in a gentler tone. "You may be the great Bishop Akpan, founder of True Faith Ministries, highly revered by people all over the country, but you aren't God. You're human, prone to illnesses, prone to weakness."

She walked over to him and sat on the floor beside him. "Take your insulin, and tell your congregation you're sorry, that you misunderstood, that you were wrong."

"What do you care?" he mumbled. "You've always thought the worst of me."

"If only you know how far off your statement is," she said, a tight knot forming in her throat. "If only."

The room became silent again except for the rather loud snores coming from the toddler on the mat. Then, her mother spoke, her soft voice as soothing as ever.

"I have made an appointment with Dr. Ekpe for Monday morning, Bishop. Should I cancel it?"

Emem noticed a fleeting clenching of her father's jaw as his lips thinned into tense lines.

"No," he muttered, his eyes still on her although he was responding to his wife's question. "I'll see what he has to say about the so-called insulin."

Emem drew in a relived breath and jumped off the floor.

"Great, Dad," she said, moving back to her seat. She noticed the appreciative smile from Ini and smiled back.

"Now, I've been dying to find out. Who owns the red Aston Martin parked outside?" she asked, keeping her tone cheery in an attempt to lighten the mood.

"It's Udo, o," Ini answered, laughing. "He used his entire year's bonus to buy that car."

"Hmm, maybe I should come back to the church," Emem teased, stroking her jaw with her finger in a theatrical way. "Apparently, being a preacher pays really well."

The room resounded with laughter. She laughed, too, glad to see that even her father, who still appeared irked, had curved his lips into an amused smirk.

"The Lord shall provide all our needs according to his riches in glory," Udo said, a playful glint in his eyes.

CHAPTER TWENTY-FIVE

Back in her hotel room, Emem rested her head on the edge of the bathtub as she allowed the soothing oils from the soapy foam to soak into her skin. The scent of citrus and eucalyptus filled the air and invigorated her senses.

She closed her eyes and let her mind drift off to the day with her family. It had turned out a lot better than she'd expected. Although her father had simmered with annoyance throughout the rest of her stay, she knew he would eventually heed the wishes of the family and take his medications. To Emem, that was all that mattered, and her mission in Port Harcourt had been accomplished.

Tomorrow, she'd visit her parents for a family luncheon once again before heading back home to Lagos. Back to her apartment. Her heart lurched at the thought. She would likely see Yomi again, maybe bump into him in the hallway or the parking lot.

'I love you. I won't ever give up.'

The words of his text message came back to her, tightening the muscles of her abdomen. Or maybe he would come pounding on her door, demanding to speak to her, his sexy dark eyes burning with determination.

Her body tingled with excitement at the thought. Could she resist him if he did? Did she even want to? Was she using her fertility problems as an excuse, a reason to avoid her true feelings for him? Was she running away from the realisation that, with Yomi, she'd found absolute happiness and acceptance of who she really was?

Her mobile phone rang, shattering her reflective thoughts. A loud splash later, foamy water fell to the floor as she sprang up from the tub and hurried out of the bathroom, grabbing the door for support as her feet slipped on the tiled floor on her way. It had to be Natalie calling. She was the only one with her new number. Unless Ini or someone from her family wanted to speak to her.

Completely nude, she dashed to her bed and picked up her phone. An unknown number. She paused, staring at the screen as it rang.

Nine-thirty p.m. Likely a wrong number call. This was a new SIM card with only a few numbers saved.

Shaking her head in annoyance at the intrusion of her peaceful bath, she let it go to voice mail.

The phone screen flashed again, and her heart crashed forcefully into her chest when she read the message.

'I'm at Habour Hotel lobby waiting for you. Love, Yomi.'

Emem blinked twice, fingers beginning to tremble. What? Yomi, here? How? When?

She redialled immediately, suddenly aware of the cool air against her naked skin.

"Hello, Emem." Yomi's deep voice resounded in her ear, spreading chill bumps over her flesh. "I'm downstairs."

Her knees wobbled as a blast of unadulterated joy exploded in her chest, and she plonked on the bed.

"Yomi ..." Her voice shook. "I ... I can't believe..."

"I need to see you, Emem. This fucking week without you has been pure hell," he rasped, his husky voice sending waves of pleasure down her spine. "If you don't come down, I'll cause a scene, start screaming like a madman, I'll make sure—"

"I'll be down in a second," she cut him off. "Let me get dressed. Just got out of the bath ..."

"Dear Lord! You're naked ..."

His raw response brought a flush to her cheeks. Had she let that information slip out on purpose? Goodness, she hadn't even seen him yet, and all the walls she'd spent the week building had come crumbling down.

"Yes," she whispered, her palm flying over her mouth to stifle the pleased giggle threatening to erupt from her.

She could almost picture Yomi's face. His eyes darkened with lust, and the muscles over his chiselled cheekbones tautened in startled seriousness. The way he looked anytime he stumbled onto her unexpected nudity in her flat.

She always preferred walking around her apartment naked during hot afternoons, and since he had the keys, he'd walked in to find her in her birthday suit on a few occasions. And every time, he'd stop, appearing stupefied for moments before rushing to her and lifting her into his arms. Although she usually grumbled in protest, she secretly loved seeing the aroused excitement in his eyes.

"I'll try not to think about you all wet and naked from a bath as I wait for you to come down," he said, his tone solemn. "We need to talk. And I need a clear head for what I have to say to you."

"Okay, see you in a bit," she murmured and hung up.

Heart beating at an erratic rate, she buzzed around the room excitedly, getting herself ready to meet the only man who had broken through her defences and made her truly fall in love.

***

Yomi's pulse skittered like a train running amok as he spotted Emem walk into the lobby, dressed in a pair of denim shorts and a red and white T-shirt. With her cropped hair damp and curly, her face freshly scrubbed and devoid of make-up, she looked very pretty and angelic. Divine.

How had he managed to go one week without seeing her, touching her? He rose from his seat, his gaze narrowed on her, everyone else disappearing from his peripheral vision.

Blood pounded across his temples as she approached him, and he had to swallow past a thick lump of emotion that had settled in his throat.

"Emem," he murmured when she got to him, his voice hoarse and unrecognisable even to his own ears.

"Yomi."

Her soft voice soothed pleasantly like a gentle stroke on his body.

They stood staring at each other for moments.

"I'm sorry, Emem—"

"I am sorry, Yomi—"

They both began at the same time, stopped, then broke into a fit of giggles.

"Let's go outside," he suggested when they had quietened.

He'd noticed the few heads from hotel guests that turned their way and didn't want an audience for what he needed to say to her. He wanted them open and honest with each other without the concern of prying eyes.

He held out a hand to her, and profound joy cascaded through him when she placed her soft palm in his.

Walking hand in hand, they strolled together out of the busy lobby and into the night. He led her away from the hotel entrance and to a side bench he'd spotted on his way in.

"Can we sit here and talk?"

She nodded and slumped onto the wooden bench. He exhaled with relief as he settled himself by her, still holding her hand.

They sat beside each other in silence. The half-moon hanging in the black skies above them, and the streetlights lining an adjoining sidewalk, provided adequate illumination, reflecting the brilliant sparkle of her eyes. In the distance, they could hear the muffled conversations of people out and about.

"So, how did you manage to find me?" she asked, turning to him.

He grinned. "I found your manager, Nnenna, who wouldn't give me your phone number because of some bullshit confidentiality rule." He rolled his eyes, and she chuckled, gladdening his heart. "But that rule didn't apply to Natalie's number, which I got from her. Then I called Natalie and hounded her until she gave me details of your whereabouts and how to reach you ... now, here I am."

"Wow, how determined," she teased, her eyes twinkling with amusement.

"Does it bother you that I tracked you down?"

She sighed, gave him a cheeky smile, and then shook her head. "No. We do need to talk."

Angling his body closer so that he faced her, he pinned her with a hopeful gaze.

"Emem, I'm sorry about the way I reacted—"

"No, Yomi, I'm the one who should be—"

"Please, let me say all I need to say first, sweetheart. I need you to understand, to believe deep in your heart that nothing, absolutely nothing, would ever make me not want to be with you. I love you."

"Oh, Yomi ..."

He placed his index finger over her lips to silence her. "Emem, I want to be honest about how I felt when I found out about your ... about ..."

"That I can't have children naturally," she said through the tender barrier of his finger.

He smiled, lifting his finger off her lips. "Yes, about that. I was immediately taken aback, confused, and honestly, deflated. Because you're the first woman who has ever made me think about babies, about having children."

Trailing his thumb over her jaw in a slow caress, he took a deep breath in, and continued. "When I found that dream suddenly snatched away from me, I panicked and lashed out. I'm sorry."

"Oh, Yomi—"

"Of course, it didn't help that your idiot ex broke the news to me." He grimaced in mock horror. "What on earth did you ever see in that buffoon, anyway?"

She flung her head back and laughed. "I've asked myself that question many times with no good answer ever coming to me."

He chuckled at her response, glad to see her in a jovial mood. "Emem, I love you, and I still want to be with you, share my life with you. We can create new dreams together ..."

"Oh, Yomi, I don't think it's fair to you," she muttered. "I don't want you giving up your dream because of me. Because of my bad decisions."

"Your past is the past. And I'm not giving up anything, I want—"

"Will you still feel the same if you know the truth about the reason why I can't have children?"

"I don't care—"

"Well, if we are ever going to move past this, I think you should know everything."

"You don't need to talk about it."

"Yes, I do, and have to." She released her hand from his and ran it down the front of her thighs. "I fell pregnant for Ejike about two years ago, but he didn't want a baby just yet. He managed to convince me that it was wrong timing because we weren't married yet."

Yomi's gut roiled. Although he didn't think he could stomach the rest of the story, knowing where it would lead, he sat still, listening, because he realised at this instant that this revelation was not just a simple show of honesty, but a form of therapy for Emem, a way to start on a clean slate with no other secrets lurking between them.

"He convinced me to abort the pregnancy," she said, her dejected tone pulling him out of his thoughts. "It killed me to actually go through with it, but back then, I was blinded by my emotions, my unwavering need to be with him. I'd left my family rather indignantly to move to Lagos with Ejike. I couldn't return as an unwed single mother and a further disgrace to my parents."

He reached for her hand, his chest burning with sorrow at her recount of painful events.

"It was supposed to be a simple procedure which involved taking a tablet and waiting until everything was over. The pharmacist had assured me that it would be easy." She pulled her bottom lip between her teeth, her fingers trembled in his. "Unfortunately, a week later, I was admitted to the intensive care unit ward of the hospital close to my work, after being found collapsed on the floor by my desk in a pool of blood. They said I'd developed complications from an incomplete abortion."

She averted her gaze from his, clearly regretful. Yomi wanted to wrap his arms around her, tell her he didn't fault her, that it could happen to anyone, but he said nothing, waiting for her to finish.

"I needed to have an emergency surgery to remove my womb to save my life. I can't ever be pregnant because I took the only chance that I'd ever had for granted."

Tears filled her eyes and spilled down her cheeks. He brushed them away gently with the pads of his thumbs.

"So, do you understand why I don't want to rope you into this mess of mine? Why it was so hard to tell you?" She gazed into his eyes. "You are a young man with all the options available to you. Do you really want to be stuck with an older woman with fertility problems for the rest of your life?"

He cupped her face in his hands, eyes burning with passion.

"You are more than your womb," he whispered hoarsely, his throat tight with tears. "You are a wonderful woman, Emem. Beautiful, intelligent, loving." He lowered his lips to hers and pressed a soft kiss against her mouth. "I didn't even need to meet you before I knew how amazing you are. I fell in love with you from the very first time I heard you on the radio, when you were just Sasha to me."

She broke into a sob, her body quaking. Gently, he drew her towards him and cradled her in his arms.

"Do you love me?" he asked in a husky whisper.

She pulled out of his embrace, her eyes trained on him. "Yes. With all my heart."

No hesitation. A fact. His heart swelled with pure joy.

"Then, let's defy the odds. Let's be the couple that allows love to lead the way, that doesn't let the expectations of others ruin their happiness. Let's just be Emem and Yomi."

"Emem and Yomi," she whispered, smiling through her tears. "I like the sound of that."

He hurled her back into his arms, kissing her forehead softly.

The gentle night breeze, propelled by tall palm trees planted close by, soothed his skin, and the slow rise and fall of her chest against him flooded his senses with satisfaction at the reality of holding her again. He'd been so worried about losing her all week.

"I love you, Emem," he whispered into her ear.

"Oh, Yomi. I love you, too."

Her warm breath on his face was the tangible sign that she was back in his life where she belonged.

EPILOGUE

A melodious piano tune greeted Yomi's ears as he strolled through the narrow hallway of the three-bedroom home he shared with his wife. He followed the pleasant sounds to the sitting room and paused by the opened door.

He watched with rapt attention as she moved her fingers gracefully across the keyboard, her face drawn in concentration, her eyes closed as she hummed along.

Cloaked in a silky white dressing gown and a white bonnet on her head, she looked like an angel here on Earth—such a poetic image.

Two years living with her, and he could never get enough of the music that welcomed him home nearly every Saturday morning whenever he returned from walking the dog.

Tiger, the furry brown terrier tucked under his arm, also appeared spellbound by the music floating around the house, wagging his tail happily in silence.

Yomi recognised the composition. *Nearer My God to Thee*—an old hymn. He sucked in a slow breath. Exactly how he felt at this moment. The extreme contentment that gripped him as he stood watching Emem hunched over the piano could only be supernatural.

Knowing that she felt the same way about him humbled him even more. She'd told him that she only played the piano when happy. The fact that she was constantly in front of the keyboard thrilled him immensely.

Grinning, he walked into the room.

"Hey, babe," he said, announcing his presence.

Emem's fingers suspended mid-air as she looked up. His chest expanded with love, watching her face light up immediately.

"My darling wife." He enjoyed saying those words out loud.

"Morning, guys," she greeted in a chirpy tone.

Tiger jumped out from under his arm, barking loudly, his tail flapping about in excitement.

"I swear, this dog is a traitor," Yomi grumbled playfully. He ambled towards Emem and brushed a kiss on her forehead. "I take him for walks and do all the hard work, bathing and grooming him. Yet, he sees you and abandons me immediately."

She laughed, lifting the little brown terrier in her arms and stroking behind his ears. "Aww... it's only because you gave him to me on my birthday. Tiger knows who he really belongs to."

"Haha," he snickered. "Yet, I'm the one who trains him, picks up after him."

She stuck out her tongue and wiggled her eyebrows mischievously. "You're responsible for that aspect of his upbringing, and I'm responsible for all the cuddles and hugs."

"Ha," he muttered, shaking his head in jest. "You and Tiger have formed a conspiracy against me."

Emem winked. "Yes, we have, haven't we, little angel?"

She brushed the terrier's thick fur again, giggling as the dog swiped his tongue repeatedly across her finger.

"Okay, Tiger, get off and let me have some time with my woman," Yomi said with feigned jealousy, lifting the dog and setting him on the floor.

They both laughed as an irate Tiger ran off to the corner of the sitting room and settled on his favourite cushion.

Sighing with contentment, Yomi sat on the wooden bench beside his wife.

Her soft floral scent rose to his nose, drawing an instant and feral response from him. A flow of warm blood rushed to his groin, filling and lifting his manhood. Gosh. Could he ever make one Saturday without attacking Emem by this piano?

He inhaled deeply, a bit embarrassed by the constant ache he had for her, the hunger that always consumed him whenever he thought about her.

Emem's presence in his life had brought him constant joy. She made him happy. Even when they disagreed—a rare occurrence—he always looked forward to coming back home to her. Two years married, and nothing had changed.

Lowering his head, he covered her mouth with his. He'd intended a quick kiss, but her hot mouth parted for him, and she swiped her keen tongue across his upper lip. His good intentions got shot to Hell.

"God, Emem," he groaned, cradling her neck, angling her head to deepen the kiss. "Can't ever get enough of you."

"Oh, Yomi," she whimpered. Her arms flew around his shoulders as she pulled him closer.

"You do this on purpose, don't you?" he rasped, his tone raw, eager fingers clutching the belt of her robe and dragging it apart until it fell away from her shoulders. "Every Saturday, you sit by this piano half-dressed, aiming to distract me."

She let out a soft giggle as she reached between them to pull his erection from his shorts. The husky sound surged like an aphrodisiac through his body, demolishing all his control, intensifying his desire.

With a harsh grunt, he grasped the top edge of her flimsy night gown and rent it down the middle, watching with fascination as her large, round breasts popped free.

"Damn," he groaned, immediately nuzzling his face against the full softness.

"Works like a charm," she whispered, sitting astride him and impaling herself on his thick shaft. "Never fails me."

"Good God!" he gasped, grabbing the plump globes of her ass as he pushed upwards into her. "You're already so wet."

"For you. Always for you."

***

Loud buzzing sounds pierced her subconscious. Emem sprang upright, disoriented in the darkness. She whipped her gaze to the flashing light of her phone on the bedside table and picked it up.

Sliding her thumb across the screen, she held the handset against her ear.

Yomi, who had also woken up, switched on the bedside lamp, his forehead furrowed in concern.

"Hello," she said, her heart in her throat. Turning to Yomi, she mouthed, "Mrs. Adeyemo."

"Madam, Anita is in labour," Dupe Adeyemo, the founder of *Angel Women*, a surrogacy agency, announced from the other end of the line.

Blood rushed to her head. The very words she'd been waiting to hear for the past few days sent her brain reeling with a mixture of excitement and trepidation.

"Oh, my God," she cried, sitting upright. "It's happening …"

"Yes, my sister," Dupe said, her tone chirpy. "The driver is on his way to St. Mary's Maternity."

Yomi was already off the bed, scrambling to the side of the door to switch on the light.

"Thank you, Mrs. Adeyemo. We are on our way," she quipped.

As soon as she ended the call, she glanced at Yomi who was now out of his night wear and in a pair of jeans and T-shirt, a travel bag in his hand.

"Wow, you really prepared adequately for this," she whispered, eyes wide in amazement.

"Yes, I practiced many times for this moment," he declared proudly, patting the bag in his hand. "Everything packed and ready."

Emem jumped up, tore out of her night gown, and quickly donned a boubou and a pair of flip flops. She scurried to the bathroom, swirled a cup of mouthwash in her mouth, spat it out, and dashed back.

Draping a scarf over her cropped hair, she gazed at the dressing mirror, her heart pounding a staccato beat in her chest. Her eyes caught Yomi's through the mirror, and she smiled at him.

He'd been awesome through it all—enduring her mood swings while she injected herself with hormones, the surgical procedure of retrieving her eggs, telling tales of the embarrassing moment of producing his sample, the stressful period of finding a surrogate, the devastation of the failed first attempt, and the joy of the successful second one. All the money they'd spent, but they'd always known it would be so worth it.

Now, they were almost there ...

"It's happening, Yomi ... it's really happening," she whispered, tears of joy blurring her vision.

"Yes, my darling wife," he murmured, his voice hoarse with emotion. "We are going to be parents."

Several hours later, she sat beside him in a private room at St. Mary's Maternity, cradling their son Tunde in her arms. His chubby cheeks moved with purpose, and his alert eyes fixed on her as he sucked on the bottle of milk in her hand.

She glanced sideways and smiled at the sleeping form of Tosin, their daughter, all bundled up in Yomi's arms. A spitting image of Yomi, with thick curly hair and a cute pointy nose, yet, she could see some of herself in the baby who had inherited her dark brown skin.

Twins. An amazing gift. Intense gratitude filled her heart. She shifted her gaze to Anita who lay on the bed, looking at them with satisfaction in her eyes.

Emem knew that members of her and Yomi's family were patiently waiting at the hospital reception for a chance to welcome the twins, but she had wanted to spend a few more minutes with the surrogate angel who had graciously offered herself to be their hope.

"Thank you for doing this for us," she said to Anita, her throat tight with tears of gratitude.

Yomi looked up and nodded his thanks to Anita but said nothing, the awe reflected in his eyes so touching as he refocused his attention on the sleeping baby in his arms.

Anita beamed at them. "You're welcome. And thank you for trusting me to carry your babies. You both look so happy. I'm confident you'll make great parents."

"Thank you, Anita."

Emem rose from her seat slowly, making sure to keep Tunde snuggled comfortably in her arms. She turned to Yomi who remained captivated, admiring their daughter. She smiled as she shook her head, already imagining the strong bond Tosin would have with her father.

"It's time to take our babies home, babe," she said to him, brushing her free palm across his shoulder.

He lifted his head, and a slow grin spread across his face. "Yes, my darling. Let's go home."

Thank you for reading!
Remember to leave a review.
Connect with Amaka Azie:
Facebook.com/AmakaAzie1
Twitter.com/AmakaAzie

OTHER BOOKS BY LOVE AFRICA PRESS

Queer and Sexy Collection Vol 1 by Eniitan

Be My Valentine Anthology Vol 1 by Amaka Azie,
Fiona Khan, Nana Prah, Sable Rose, Empi Baryeh

His Captive Princess by Kiru Taye

Dawsk by Erhu Kome Yellow

CONNECT WITH US

Facebook.com/LoveAfricaPress

Twitter.com/LoveAfricaPress

Instagram.com/LoveAfricaPress

www.loveafricapress.com